CRUEL HATE

A COLLEGE SPORTS ROMANCE

HIDDEN VALLEY ELITE
BOOK FIVE

ISLA VAUGHN

ARROWSCOPE PRESS, LLC

Cruel Start

(p) ISBN-13: 978-1-951919-65-8

(e) ISBN-13: 978-1-951919-57-3

Cruel Hate

(p) ISBN-13: 978-1-951919-49-8

(e) ISBN-13: 978-1-951919-48-1

Publisher: Arrowscope Press, LLC; www.arrowscopepress.com

Editing— Kate B., Amanda K., Line Editor, Taylor A., Kristina B., Proofreader, Angie G., Beta Reader, Red Adept Editing

Cover Design—T.E. Black Designs; www.teblackdesigns.com

Interior Formatting & Design— Arrowscope Press, LLC; www.arrowscope-press.com

AUTHOR NOTE

I'm so excited for you to get to know Phoenix and Aspen. Their story begins with the prequel to their duet, Cruel Start. I'm including it here as bonus content. This duet is a college sports romance with plenty of angst.

Enjoy!

Isla Vaughn

CRUEL START

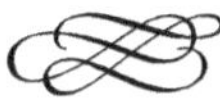

A COLLEGE SPORTS ROMANCE

CHAPTER ONE

PHOENIX

"Move, Phoenix." Tracey's annoying voice interrupted my moment of peace, and clawlike fingers waved in front of my face.

Another group of people poured into the backyard, where brats and burgers still scented the air. The impromptu barbecue had turned into a full-blown party.

"You're blocking my sun."

I tensed from the volume of Tracey's shrill voice as she competed to be heard over the music and laughter. "You sure about that? If I do, you might burst into flames. Not unlike when you step foot in a church," I snarled but scooted slightly out of her sun's path, half wishing that she would spontaneously combust.

Her top lip peeled back, showing me her perfectly straight, clenched teeth. "If you weren't Shane's brother…"

They were all so whipped. My brother was almost as bad as Cole. All three of them—Cole, Damon, and Shane—had been snared. Not me. I wasn't about to let some girl sidetrack me— which is exactly what Damon, Cole, and Shane all said before they got whipped. Idiots. My future had too much at stake, and a girl would only complicate things. It wasn't like I didn't like Riley, Skylar, and Tracey—well, Tracey not so much—but they changed everything and made me the odd man out.

"Finish the thought, Trace. What would you do?"

"Phoenix!" Shane yelled from across the yard. "We're getting a game going. Come over here, and stop flirting with my girlfriend."

I grimaced. I think I just threw up in my mouth at that end-of-day suggestion. Riley snorted, and I winked at her. She got my vibe about Tracey.

"Want to play, Riles? Bet Cole and I could convince the guys to do flag instead of tackle."

She flicked her long dark-brown hair over her shoulder, placing a hand on her hip. "Thanks, but no. Smith and Jameson are over there, and I don't trust them to play by the rules."

"Which ones are they?" I shielded my eyes as I scanned the group of guys near my brother.

"The mammoth tree-sized ones."

"Ahh, gotcha." I didn't know those guys, and if something happened to Riley, I wouldn't forgive myself. "Come cheer us on."

She laughed but grabbed Skylar and followed until they found a spot on the grass to watch. Tracey trailed behind them at a leisurely pace, casting longing glances at the group around the firepit roasting marshmallows on skewers. She tossed her oversized bag on the ground before sitting a little ways away from the girls.

The summer was almost halfway over. We'd spent most of our free time hanging out at the cove, surfing, training, and the occasional barbeque.

I felt alive, exhilarated. Preseason football practice at the college would start soon. My brother and I were spending the weekend at our cousin Cole's house near Thane University—which would soon be our home.

Putting the black-souled demon from my thoughts, I slapped my brother on the back. "We doin' this?"

We lined up on the freshly mowed grass of Thane University's football house. The back and side yard were big, relatively flat, and ideal for a pickup game. I lived and breathed football, had for as long as I could remember, and my dream to play in the NFL was almost within reach. It was the perfect "fuck you" to my dad, a mediocre tight end on Chicago's team who had deserted our mom when she was pregnant with us. I was a better athlete than him. So was Shane. Revenge was almost in our grasp.

It was hot as hell out with the sun directly overhead, but that didn't stop us. It took minutes to split up into teams and get the game underway. We played with a handful of Cole's teammates who'd returned early, like he and Riley, who were both sophomores, had. And when they'd invited us for the weekend, my brother and Damon, Cole's brother, had piled into a car and driven up.

Several girls had joined—Riley, Skylar, and Tracey, Shane's steady girlfriend—to cheer us on. Riley and Skylar were sitting on the grass and talking while Tracey read a magazine, not bothering to be a part of the group. I blocked out all the distractions—girls—and focused on the game.

Carter snapped the ball to me, setting the play in motion. The offense held back the defensive players that tried to rush me while I surveyed the field to target a receiver. The offense and defensive lines collided. Damon was open. I launched the ball, sidestepping Matt's late tackle. Damon stretched out a hand, Evan on his heels, and grabbed the ball out of the air, tucking it into his side as he sprinted to our makeshift end zone. Evan tackled him, taking Damon to the ground. When Evan shifted off him, Damon popped back to his feet, dropping the football where he'd landed.

The defensive line was stacked with several huge juniors,

and I eyed them warily. The next play went off without a hitch. I threw the ball down the field, and we gained a first down, thanks to Cole's catch and quick feet.

We lined up. Carter snapped the ball. No one was open. I shifted my weight to the balls of my feet to sprint as the offensive line was overrun. The hit was blinding, and I crashed into the grass. One of the tree trunks, Jameson I think, rolled off me. He gained his feet, offering me a hand. I took it, shaking out the cobwebs. That was a hell of a hit. I rolled my shoulders and got back into position, ready to go again.

The ball was snapped. Our line held, and I found Shane. I threw for a long pass, a brick to his chest that he caught with ease—until Smith, a six-foot-three and two-hundred-seventy-five-pound linebacker, tackled him, and the ball bounced free. The loud pop when they collided echoed ominously through my soul. Then silence fell over the field. It had never sounded so loud, and I knew something terrible had happened.

Smith got up. Shane did not.

Cole and Damon got to him first. I sprinted to where my brother lay on the field, taking assurance that his eyes were open. He was conscious. *It can't be that bad, right?* God, I hoped not.

I should have spoken up when the debate for the game had ensued. While my cousins had agreed with Shane and me that it would be fine to play tackle, some of the other guys weren't too sure. It was before the season. *What if someone got hurt?* I thought it would be okay. *Why did we tempt fate?*

I dropped to the grass beside my brother. His arm was at an awkward angle. *Fuck.* "How bad does it feel?"

"Hurts like hell, but I'm fine." Shane grimaced.

"Gotta say, bro, I'm glad we don't have that weird twin thing because it looks painful."

"Piss off. Help me up."

That was my surly brother. A sliver of reassurance pushed

the dread away as I reached for his good arm to help him up. Cole supported Shane's right arm as he rolled onto his feet. His injured limb dangled by his side, even with Cole's aid.

"That doesn't look good." I hated to say it for many reasons, one being that our mom would find out and panic.

As an ER nurse, she hadn't been crazy about us coming up to blow off some steam before we officially moved. She'd said she had a bad feeling about it. She was right.

"You know we'll have to go to the hospital." I rubbed the back of my neck. "And Mom will hear about it."

Shane scowled, some of the pain obscured by his frown lines. "You call her."

I didn't bother arguing with him as we slowly walked to where I'd parked. Sky and Riley rushed over, Tracey not far behind.

"We're going with," Sky said.

She slid into the car with Damon while I helped Shane into the passenger seat.

Cole tapped the roof of my SUV after I got Shane settled. "Riley and I'll meet you there. We can take Tracey." He glanced to where she'd hung back with Smith and a few other guys.

"No"—Tracey's half smile was weak—"I'll grab a ride. I can talk to Shane later."

I shoved the anger at her response deep into my gut. I bet she would find a ride, and it would be with one of the guys we'd played with. I'd caught her flirting more than once, but Shane was oblivious. God, I hated her.

Shane's grimace jerked me back to how much pain he was in. The urgency I'd felt since he'd hit the ground came back in a rush. I pulled onto the street and took the shortest route to the hospital. Cole followed.

By the time we got there, parked, and waited for our turn, an hour had passed before we saw a doctor. He looked close to retirement with white hair and a bushy mustache that seemed to have a personality of its own, a stoic one.

"Good afternoon. I'm Dr. Mathews." His caterpillar eyebrows climbed his forehead. "There's an awful lot of you. How about some wait in the—oh." Recognition sparked in his faded-blue eyes as he paused on Cole. "I know you. You made that interception and ran the field last homecoming. Damn good player. Keep that up, and you have a promising career ahead of you."

"Thank you, sir."

Cole nodded then shifted his gaze pointedly to Shane, whose frown only deepened the longer he sat immobile on the stark-white hospital bed.

"I'll go out on a limb here and guess this is a football injury?" the doc inquired.

Shane mumbled a response then clenched his teeth against the poking and prodding as the doctor examined him. I shifted from foot to foot, uncomfortable with the amount of pain bracketing his mouth.

"Your shoulder is dislocated. I will pop it back in." The doc's bushy mustache barely moved as his lips formed each word. "You'll be in a sling for a few weeks then PT, but you should be fine to play after that."

The nurse ushered everyone out as they got ready to set Shane's dislocated shoulder back into its socket. I refused to go.

The doc maneuvered Shane's arm into a ninety-degree posi-tion by holding his wrist, guiding the bone back into the shoulder socket. It gave a small pop. I shivered at the sound and Shane's audible grunt of discomfort. They fastened a sling around his neck and arm and pressed ice against his shoulder. Once finished, the doctor left, and the nurse said she would be back with the discharge paperwork, physical therapy orders, and instructions.

I slumped into the chair by his bed when it was just us. One look at his drawn face, and I knew how much it weighed on him that Tracey wasn't by his side. I would never understand how my idiot brother couldn't see what she was all about.

"Hey"—I leaned forward, elbows to knees—"if you have to sit out a few games, it's no big deal."

"That's bullshit, and you know it."

Yeah, it was, but I kept my mouth shut. We had four years, but to both of us, not playing was like getting a limb cut off.

"I better not lose Tracey over this."

My brother had a one-track mind. The bitch still wasn't there yet. But Shane's words gave me an idea. "I'm gonna make that call to Mom."

"Better you than me." Shane shot me a sinister grin.

I left the room and headed toward the stairs, pushing aside the call I said I would make to Mom. I needed to intercept Tracey.

A little white lie just might be the thing to extract her teeth from my brother.

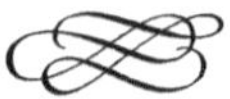

CHAPTER TWO

ASPEN

"This shit is ridiculous." Regan buried her face in the futon's cushion and let out a muffled scream.

"Right?"

Like always, she summed it up so eloquently. We exchanged weary glances. My year-younger sister rubbed her temples, no doubt trying to stave off the headache from listening to Mom and Dad scream at each other.

"They're arguing like they have a million dollars' worth of shit to fight over instead of a couple of cars and us."

Regan sat up and snorted. "And you don't even count anymore. You leave for college soon."

"Like you count?"

Regan hadn't been home more than a few days a week since school had ended. I knew she was couch surfing, and I felt terrible to be abandoning her that fall. She had a great group of friends and a boyfriend who would walk across fire for her, but I still felt like I should be there to deflect the worst of our parents.

"Will you be okay?"

"Please, sis." She rolled her eyes. "I'm not going to be a pawn in their game. I'll barely be home, since I'm going to stay at Dane's once school starts. Thank God the 'rents agreed to that."

I was surprised they had. Regan and Dane had been together for two years. Since we moved a few months ago, at the end of the year, she would have had to change schools, but his parents had offered her a room for her senior year. She was so much better off with them anyway.

"Before you know it, I'll be graduating and heading to New York with Dane."

"Well"—I pushed out a guilt-heavy breath—"the dorms at Thane are outrageously expensive. But I'll have an apartment next year, so you'll have somewhere to live if you need a place to go."

Regan flipped her long blond hair over her shoulder before lifting herself onto the kitchen counter. We'd been holed up there for the past couple of hours, as we had nowhere else to go in the tiny two-bedroom, government-subsidized rental. It was the only thing our parents could afford after losing our house when Dad lost his job and discovered Mom had substantial credit card debt, which, when added to his, was insurmountable. That disaster had resulted in our parents' farce of a divorce that still found them fucking then turning around to fight over who'd started it.

"Seriously, Aspen. Dane will make buttloads of cash when he graduates and joins his dad's architectural firm."

I fought against the eye roll that needed to punctuate her statement. She was so young. "What if things don't work out between you guys? Or if his parents think you're mooching off him?"

Dane's family was wealthy, and they had a condo in New York, where Dane and Regan planned to live while they went to college. Regan would go for fashion design and merchandizing not far from Dane's school, which she had a full ride for, thanks to the Future of Fashion contest she'd won. Intelligence was the only thing our parents gave us that I was grateful for. Despite their fucked-up lives, they were brilliant, but they were stupid regarding love and impulsive money decisions. It had taught me more than my starry-eyed sister. I didn't believe in love. And I was very good with money.

"Stop questioning me." Regan pulled me from my thoughts. "You leave in a few weeks for Thane, and our parents have no money to help. Are you sure you'll be okay?"

"Please." I played it off. "I've got that waitressing gig, and"—I pretended to buff my nails on my shirt then looked at them as if each finger held a shiny new diamond—"I've got scholarships that'll cover everything." Except for books and rent, but I kept that to myself.

Regan hopped off the counter, flinching as the shouting went up another couple of decibels. The sound of shattering glass followed. "I'm out of here. Going to Dane's to save my sanity and eardrums."

I grabbed the bag I'd stashed on the screened-in back porch for times like that. "Me too."

We didn't bother leaving a note. They wouldn't even know we were gone. Regan and I had beater cars, the only things our parents had done to save us from their colossal fights. When they'd bought new vehicles, they'd kept their old ones and gifted them to us. We had to pay for gas, repairs, and insurance, but it meant freedom, an escape.

I turned the key in my ignition and almost sagged with relief as the engine turned over with a grumble. My sister cackled before starting her powder-blue Toyota.

I pointed at her, giving her the stink eye. "You did the same thing."

"Better believe it. I'm on a first-name basis with the car gods."

Sadly, I agreed with her on that one. I waved then backed up, pointing my rusty bucket of bolts and barely working engine toward the cove. I could've painted or gone surfing, but I needed something truly freeing, and plummeting to my possible death tended to win out in times like that. Besides, it was the only thing that quieted the anger inside me.

I wanted to drive to Deleon's Cliff, but the cove at the state park was closer to our home—if I could call it that—and would be better on my gas tank and dwindling cash supply. The cove wasn't Deleon's, but it would do. It was a cliff with water beneath it, I supposed, and that was all I needed it to be.

Time flew as I got lost in my thoughts, and I was at the cove before I knew it. The roads curved around beautiful reddish-brown cliffs, offering peeks of the blue river that fed into the cove. I pulled into the small lot to park, grabbed my bag, and tossed my keys inside.

Once at the trail that led to where I would jump, I peeled off my shirt and shimmied out of my soft cotton shorts to reveal the one-piece bathing suit I'd had on since getting dressed that morning, then I shoved the rest of my clothes into my backpack and looped the strap over my shoulder. When I came to a cluster of bushes at the first bend in the path, I stowed my bag and jogged up to the fifty-foot cliff, glancing covetously at the neighboring seventy-foot drop. *Someday.* And with how my parents were interacting, probably sooner than later.

Like always, I toed the cliff's edge and felt no fear. I had no reason to. Only success or death waited for me on the other side of the dive, and I wasn't afraid of the latter.

I pushed off. Then I was free-falling through the air with that addictive sense of freedom and weightlessness. I hit the water with a small splash and was enveloped in another world. Silence followed as I kicked to the surface and swam to shore. I'd jumped there about twenty-five times since we'd moved.

I'd climbed back to my spot on the rocky ledge when my morbid mind intervened, and I glanced at the jagged rock two feet to the left. A part of me wondered, *If I miss my mark, would anyone give a fuck if I land there, my brains splattered on the rocks below?*

I rubbed my hands over my face, desperate to expel thoughts of death. The recent memory of my parents screaming didn't help, which was why I needed to stop thinking and just jump. So I did, several more times, exhausting myself in the process.

My lack of fear had another benefit. I rocked cliff-diving competitions. The prize money helped to fund my get-out-of-Dodge stash. Swimming to shore, I squeezed the water out of my hair before retrieving my backpack. The towel inside went around my waist, and I looped my arm through the strap, satisfied that I'd pushed away the bad thoughts. I would live to dive another day, thanks to the clear head diving gave me.

I headed to my car while digging through my bag to find my keys. *Why are they always at the bottom and so difficult to find?* What I wouldn't give for one of those key fobs that unlocked the doors just by being near it. My fingers closed around the metal key ring just as I slammed into something hard. Dazed, I stumbled back, one hand reaching out so I didn't fall.

Strong hands grabbed my arms, steadying me. Panicked, I snapped my gaze toward who had ahold of me and locked eyes with the hottest guy I'd ever seen. *Holy shit.* Of their own accord, my fingers curled against warm, muscular ridges. *He's fucking gorgeous.*

I mumbled sorry, but it got stuck in my throat, and I choked as a sexy grin pulled at his mouth. The heat of his hands fell away. My brain short-circuited from how handsome he was, and I couldn't look away. His lips moved, forming words, but I couldn't process them. My gaze bounced over his chiseled face, blond hair, a to-die-for athletic body, and those silvery, hypnotic eyes.

I swiped at some wetness at the side of my mouth. *Oh my god, is that drool?*

Heat rushed over my face. It was enough to free me from his

hot-guy trance, and I quickly sidestepped him, hurrying to my car so I wouldn't be late for work.

But the warmth of his hand on my body and those eyes, an impossible silver, stayed with me as I got into my car and sped away. A mouthwatering fantasy made me want to turn the car around.

My gaze jumped to the rearview mirror because I had to know—*Is he standing there, watching me?*

CHAPTER THREE

PHOENIX

Even the best sandwich I'd ever made wasn't good enough to get my mind off the girl from the cove and how I hadn't gotten laid in way too long. But it would have to do.

I'd just taken a bite when the door slammed, and my five-kinds-of-mopey brother stormed through the house. He tossed his keys on the counter, and everything clicked into place. Tracey still hadn't been around or taken him to physical therapy like he'd assured me would happen after the text and voice mail he'd left her earlier.

Mom had a night shift at the ER and was already gone after fretting over Shane for a solid hour. She'd been upset she couldn't take him. I would've driven him, but he'd had other ideas—that hadn't worked.

I'd tried to talk to him about the she-devil at least a thousand times, but he'd been a big crybaby. So fuck it—I would rub it in. "How was PT? Tracey didn't stick around after taking you?" I yelled at his retreating back.

He stopped, rounded the corner back into the kitchen, and gave me a glare from the depths of hell. "How do you think it fucking was?" He lifted his arm, the one in the sling, winced, and eased it down. "And no. She didn't."

"She's a bloodsucker, bro. Do yourself a favor, and cut her loose." Although, it was probably—hopefully—too late for that, as she hadn't come around or called him since the accident.

"Shut up." Shane stormed toward his room. The door slammed a minute later.

Progress. I swiveled back to the island to finish my sandwich.

Shane normally got defensive when I said anything remotely close to how evil she was. Not that time. The floor started thumping to the beat of the music he turned on at the highest level. I raised my glass to him, toasting the start of him letting her go. *He's better off without her.* Everyone knew she was down to marry a superstar money-making athlete—NFL, MLB, FIFA. It didn't matter to her, so long as she was on that train. Why my brother had been blind to it was a mystery.

The conversation I'd had with her before she'd even crossed the threshold into the hospital came to mind in perfect clarity. I'd raced to the entrance. Thank fuck for the text Cole sent warning that he'd spotted the she-devil in the parking lot and that she was on her way.

"Tracey." I skidded to a halt as the hospital doors slid closed behind me and did a quick scan of the lot to see who she'd ridden in with. I couldn't tell—probably a good thing. "I'm glad I caught you."

She narrowed her eyes at me, popping a hand on her jutted hip bone. "What room is Shane in?"

I pushed out a weary breath and tried to appear sad, rubbing a hand over my forehead and hanging my head. "He doesn't want to see anyone. Well, he can't anyway."

"What are you talking about?" Her shoulders bunched, and she leaned forward slightly.

I could tell she was going to shove me to the side, or try to, if I didn't put a fast stop to it. "He's not doing well. The injury is bad. At the very least he'll redshirt this season. That is, if he can play again."

"You're lying." But she eased back, her brow scrunched. "It was just a hit. He takes them on the field all the time."

"Yeah, but not against guys the size of the tank that almost tore his arm off. Well, he did tear something, and it may not be operable. If they can't do anything for him, he'll go to PT and try to get the most mobility he can from it. After... well, I don't know what to say. I shouldn't even be telling you this. He didn't want you to know. Said to tell you he'll be fine."

"I'm going to see him." She stepped to the side.

I'd mirrored her move. "You can't. The doc gave him something to knock him out. The pain's bad. And he didn't want you to see him like this."

A flash of sunlight temporarily blinded me, bringing me back to the present. After blinking the spots from my eyes, I saw a car had pulled into the driveway—and specifically who owned that car as they walked toward the front door. *Shit, that's Tracey.* I jumped out of my seat and went to the door, yanking it open before she had a chance to ring the bell.

The bitch wasn't getting in. I would do whatever it took to protect my brother, even if he blamed me later when he inevitably found out. Because that was the thing with secrets. They never stayed buried where they should. *Still worth it.*

"Hey, Trace." I injected a note of remorse into my voice, softening it to throw her off-balance.

"Get out of my way, Phoenix." She pulled her ponytail forward to hang over her chest in a flow of golden blond. "I'm here to see Shane."

That was the annoying she-devil's catchphrase.

"Yeah." I rubbed the back of my neck, glancing cautiously over my shoulder and inside the house. "That's the thing. He's not doing great, and I'm not sure you should be here right now. It'll only make things worse."

Her head jerked back, and she tensed. "What's that supposed to mean? He said he was fine."

"Remember I told you he'd say that?"

She frowned, and I pushed ahead with the lie.

"Look, he got some horrible news from the doc."

"Is he out the season?" Red infused her cheeks, and her hands curled into fists as she stepped closer. "This is all your fault."

"How's that? I'm not the one who hit him." *Where did she get her logic?*

"You threw him the ball when that tree trunk of a man was right there. You wanted him to get hurt so you could be the star and have all the attention from the coach and get picked for an NFL team over him." She crossed her arms over her fake tits. "I told him you would pull something like this."

She was off her rocker. When she took another step forward, I held out my hand, palm up. I couldn't let her inside, and no way was I going to address her brand of crazy. It would only get worse if I fed into it. I would be the first to admit that winding her up could be fun as hell but not when I wanted her to leave quickly.

"The doc said Shane's pro career was over before it started. The damage to his shoulder is too extensive to be repaired."

"Ah." She took a half step back, her mouth hanging open. Seconds ticked by. "I thought he had PT. Are they sure?"

"Yeah, he does, but it won't change things. And he's in a shit mood, but—"

A calculating gleam flashed in her baby blues, giving a glimpse into her dark soul before she whirled around, not even waiting for me to finish. A second later, she was in her car, pulling out of the driveway and onto the road. Once her car was out of sight, I let loose the laughter I'd been holding in.

He'll forgive me... eventually. If he never found out, all the better. But otherwise, I hoped he learned about it much later and after he'd had someone else underneath him.

I went back inside, finished my homework, then pounded on Shane's door, yelling at him to watch the game. I needed to keep him busy and his mind far from calling Tracey. The music shut off, and soon, we were both settled on the couch in front of our aging TV. Halfway through the game, he got a text.

"Motherfucker." Shane launched his phone across the room. It hit the wall with an ominous *thump*.

"What world-ending news did you just get?" Seriously, his theatrics lately were getting on my last nerve. But I was trying. If I lost football, or even half a season, I knew I would go crazy too.

"That was Tracey." Shane's voice cracked, and I sat up straight. "She broke up with me."

"In a text." I knew she was a bitch, but that was all kinds of low after they'd dated for two years. "There's a party at the cove tonight. Our cousin will be there. Let's go." I needed to do something to take his mind off her, and I hoped to find some fun, or trouble. As long as I kept my scholarship, I didn't care about anything else.

CHAPTER FOUR

ASPEN

The sun beat down, heating my skin and drying little droplets of water. I leaned back on my arms and tilted my face to the sky. At the cliff's edge, Erin shrieked as she jumped. A shiver of anticipation propelled me to stand, and the rough rock bit into the soles of my feet. I wanted to go again.

I could still hear Erin just before she hit the water. She screeched every time, and I swore it was to get attention. I didn't bother to watch. Drama followed that one. And while I was thrilled I'd found my people at the new cove, I didn't mesh well with a few. She was one.

We'd been meeting up for two weeks in the afternoons before my dinner shift at the diner to cliff dive. Most of us tandem jumped. I'd already gone with the group, but Jack and Erin were climbing out of the water for another go, and Aaron had stopped me from taking a turn with a hand on my wrist. He thought it would be cool if we all picked spots on the cliff and went at once. Good with it, I took the opportunity to scan the area below to peek at a few cars that had pulled up.

For a while, I'd held out hope that the hottie I'd run into the other day would make another appearance. Then I could make a better impression. Sadly, he hadn't. I was over it.

"Did you hear about the party happening here today?" Aaron nudged me with his bony shoulder.

Ah, that's why all the cars. "No, but I'm up for a party. Is it just our group?" On any given day, seven to ten of us adrenaline junkies were feeding our addiction. And aside from the bullshit going on at home—the parents' pending divorce, sleeping together, then even louder fights—I was glad we'd moved. The cliffs were better, and I'd found my tribe.

It wasn't terrible for my sis either. She just spent more time at Dane's house. His parents adored her, and she would move in when school started and I left. Our parents would hardly know she was gone. They were so fucked up.

That was all good, but it didn't stop the worry, the bone-chilling hollowness that ate at my soul. The other day, Dad was shouting at Mom about how different his life would have been if she hadn't trapped him. But she'd gotten pregnant, and that was where his dreams had died. *Thanks for that, Dad.*

Growing up, they'd both drilled into our heads how impor-tant it was to use protection—we were eleven and ten, respec-tively, for that first conversation. They'd said it was better to stay a virgin, to wait, and not take any chances until we were ready for marriage. My sis had sex after her first month of dating Dane. They were almost sixteen. She said it was the best decision she'd ever made because she knew she would marry the guy someday. After two years and watching how crazy in love they were, I thought she might be right.

Not me. I'd held onto my V-card. I was firmly in the camp that marriage was not for me. Frankly, all our parents' shouting and mixed signals with the angry makeup sex—shudder— messed with my head. However, I wasn't convinced holding out was such a good idea anymore.

A car door slammed, then another, and I knew the party Aaron had mentioned was underway below. It had everyone so jacked up, anticipation thick in the air. Aaron directed two of the guys to higher ledges. I took my usual place at the fifty-foot main outcropping. A big group of people had congregated near the edge of the water and fanned out along the open area at the base of the cliffs, where a few picnic tables and a small pavilion were located.

Music infiltrated the space, wafting up to us as we perched on the cliff at various heights. Instead of focusing on all the people below, I pictured the jump and when my body would meet the water. Then Aaron blew the foghorn, and suddenly, hundreds of eyes looked at us as we leaped in tandem.

The familiar thrill rushed through me. All my problems dissolved in that moment of freedom. Then the water welcomed me into its muted, murky abyss. Kicking to the surface, I swam to the shore with my group. We rose from the water to a crowd not impressed with what we'd done. They'd gone back to drinking and partying. I brushed off the lack of enthusiasm. It probably wasn't the first time they'd seen something like that at what appeared to be a well-used party spot.

It was nearing dusk and not a good idea to attempt any more dives off the cliff. I grabbed my towel and ran it over my legs before pulling shorts out of my bag and shimmying into them. I spotted Erin by a group of girls, and when our gazes met, she waved me over. I could use more friends, so I went.

"Aspen, this is Piper, Teagan, and Tracey." Erin gestured to three girls, who resembled lifelike Barbies with their flawless makeup, sparkly diamonds, and fake smiles. "I went to Hidden Valley Academy with them."

Lovely. They were from the rich kids' high school. I flashed a smile I didn't feel, but I could pretend with the best of them. No way would I disclose that I went to public school at Hidden Valley High. It was better to redirect the conversation to the future, not linger in a past where the snobs would find me lacking. "Hi. Are you guys going to Thane in August?"

Piper's forehead crinkled the tiniest bit as she scrutinized me. "You look familiar."

I shook my head. "My family moved here not too long ago. I doubt we've met."

She shrugged, dropping it. "Tracey and I are going to Thane, but Teagan's headed to New York for fashion."

I nodded. The world would soon have another designer who didn't care about the environment, because Teagan looked like someone who wouldn't use sustainable resources or fabric dyed with methods in harmony with the planet.

Tracey flicked her flaxen hair so it fell down her back and sneered off into the distance directly over my shoulder. The other girls followed her gaze. Teagan threaded her arm through Tracey's, concern etched on her features, then murmured that it was time for them to go. Piper looked on with amusement as the two from her group made a hasty retreat. Erin's eyes grew wide, and Piper's snapped back to mine.

"Don't mind them." Piper's grin widened. "Messy break up with that one's brother."

I looked over my shoulder and froze like prey caught in a predator's line of sight. *It's him.* My heart kicked into overdrive with an added shot of adrenaline. *Holy hell.* He was even hotter than I remembered.

An electric bolt sizzled between us. He strolled toward me, a wicked half smile curving lips I wanted to taste more than my next breath. Lust coiled low in my belly, and my pulse kicked up another notch. Nothing about him was soft as he moved, his muscles shifting and bunching. My fingers curled at my sides, and I wondered if it would be too forward if I leaped onto him like a koala on a branch. If anyone was going to corrupt me, I wanted it to be him.

A beer dangled from his fingertips, the same hand that had a secure grasp on a bottle of whiskey, and a wave of heat swept through me as I remembered the feel of his hands on my arms, so strong and sure. Tantalizing ideas formed the longer I looked at him. My reasons for holding out weren't worth it. Even my younger sister wasn't a virgin. And I would rather not be one going into my freshman year at Thane.

"Pipes." He spoke to Piper but didn't take his eyes off me. "Corrupting the new girl already?"

"Phoenix." Her gaze crawled all over him. "I would love a good corrupting."

He threw his head back, and the deep laugh that followed delivered a full-body shiver. No girl in hearing distance would be immune. My lips curved into a crooked grin. I wasn't in the market for a boyfriend, but the obvious bad boy was right up my alley. And I could use a distraction from what I would go home to.

"Rain check, Pipes."

She shrugged, but her eyes remained heated and on him, even as she spoke to me. "Lucky girl. Enjoy him, Aspen."

Phoenix passed me the beer dangling from his fingertips, and I took it, shifting my towel to the crook of my elbow. Though I wasn't a big drinker, I needed liquid courage for what I was about to do. He hooked his fingers with mine and pulled me from the small group.

"Do everything that I would," Piper singsonged as we walked away, and Phoenix snorted.

He drew me away from the crowd, and I followed, unable to resist. The truth was, I wouldn't have even if I could've. I needed this after the last few months I'd endured, not to mention the uncertainty I would soon face in college, making ends meet where my scholarships didn't cover and with zero help from my family. So for once, I would do the irresponsible thing and sleep with the guy I couldn't stop thinking about.

We paused on the outskirts of the party, not too far if I

changed my mind. But I knew I wouldn't. I put the beer to my lips, tipped it back, and guzzled half its contents.

"Easy there, surfer girl." Phoenix's hand settled on my hip.

"I haven't had anything to drink yet. I'll be fine." I craned my neck to take in his expression. I hadn't had anything to eat either—the fridge was empty at home—but he didn't need to know that. "And surfer girl?"

He shrugged a broad shoulder, and I enjoyed the ripple of muscle.

"You look like one, with the towhead blond. I don't know." He took a swig from the whiskey bottle. "Something about you makes me think you're at home on the waves."

I smirked. "I am." He had no idea how much at home I was out there. If I could make a living doing both those things, I would. Someday, I hoped to make my way to Hawaii, where the real competition was.

"Did you just move here?" He glanced over my shoulder at a commotion.

It sounded like Piper was arguing with a guy. I shifted to look, but Phoenix clasped my hand in his.

"Let's go for a walk."

Rather than say anything, I went along.

"You didn't answer my question. Are you new around here?"

"Yeah, I've been here a couple of months. I won't be here for long."

We followed one of the trails that led around the back of the cliff. I hadn't been there yet and took in the small, hidden grove set back from where we were. The farther we walked, the more the party noises faded. I should be nervous about going somewhere alone with a stranger, but his confident strength quieted my nerves and made me feel safe.

"Where are you going if you won't be here for long?" he asked.

"I'll be at Thane University in a few weeks."

We stopped in a tiny clearing that had privacy from the trail with a few natural boulders and bushes and sat near the partial shelter of a spindly tree.

"Are you a freshman?" He released my hand to tuck a few strands of stray hair behind my ear.

His fingers trailed along my cheek, and I shivered at how sparks seemed to jump from his touch, making me hyperaware of him. My gaze fell to his lips, and I licked mine. *What would it feel like if he kissed me?* I wanted to experience it and moved half a step closer. The heat of his body radiated into me, chasing away the slight chill that dusk had brought to the air.

"What about you?"

He had to be in college, too, judging by the sheer size and muscle development. I couldn't imagine that at about six foot two, the guy was enrolled at the academy.

"I'll be a freshman at Thane too." He leaned in, only inches from my mouth. Silvery eyes flicked briefly to mine before returning to my lips. "I want to kiss you. That okay?"

"Mm-hmm."

I tilted my chin, then his lips were on mine. Soft at first, coaxing, teasing. When mine parted on a moan, he took full advantage and slipped his tongue inside to tangle with mine. His hand gripped in the back of my wet hair, tugging and angling my head for better access and control over my mouth. I gave it to him, wanting the same.

He tasted of whiskey, with a hint of mint on his tongue, and freedom. I wanted all of him, and I didn't care that we barely knew each other. That made it even more exciting. His finger hooked beneath the strap of my bathing suit, and he slowly eased it off my shoulder. I shivered in anticipation. I was really doing it.

He peeled off my strap, cupped my breast with one hand, and squeezed it. I gasped as sensations burst through my body, and I ground my hips against him. He growled, breaking the kiss. I arched my back as he trailed kisses down my neck and to the hollow at the base of my throat, his husky words whispering over my skin.

"I want to slide inside you, surfer girl."

He released my hair, and I nodded as he pinched and rolled my nipple.

"Gonna need to hear the words, Aspen."

Some hazy part of my alcohol-infused mind realized he knew my name, making it even easier for me to do what I wanted. "Yes. I want you inside me too."

A burst of hot air fanned my heated flesh, and with deft fingers, he removed the rest of my clothes. I swayed on my feet, shivering as he released me to grab my discarded beach towel. With a flick of his wrists, it was spread on the ground before he herded me toward it.

"You're beautiful. You know that? When you jumped from the cliff then came out of the water like a fucking siren, everyone else faded. It's only been you from that moment."

I mumbled something unintelligible but understood what he meant. When I'd first seen him, something similar had happened to me.

I couldn't take my eyes off him as he slid his jeans over his hips and down to his ankles before kicking them off. Black boxer briefs did little to hide the large bulge that made my heart skip into overdrive, banging against my chest like a convict desperate for freedom. I glided forward and trailed a finger along his hardness, a thrill dancing through me when it jerked at my touch. I loved that I had power over him too. Maybe not much, but enough.

Then the last scrap of clothing that hid him from me was gone, and I swayed at his size, a sliver of anxiety piercing the haze of lust. I might have gotten myself in over my head.

He advanced, and I shivered. All thoughts fled as he grabbed my wrist and turned me so my back was against his chest. Then he was touching me. So many sensations had my mind on over-load. All I could do was feel as he held my breasts, grazed my pussy, then dipped between my legs, feeling how wet I was for him. My face heated at the way I squirmed against his touch.

His other hand trailed across my stomach until he wrapped it around my neck, holding me immobile but not too tight so that I couldn't breathe. It was the most erotic thing I'd ever experienced as he swirled his fingers in my heat, teasing my clit until I cried out. My skin was overheated, my legs weak, and I knew that if he didn't stop, I would come.

"Don't stop." I wanted to come.

"Not yet."

His deep, hoarse voice brought me closer to the edge, and I moaned. He stopped what he was doing, and my legs almost buckled from the loss of his grip on my neck and pussy. I wobbled like a baby giraffe, drunk on desire, before strong, calloused hands found my hips, and he guided me onto the towel, easing me down so my back was on the damp cotton.

"Are you protected?"

I nodded, my mind fuzzy with desire. When he wasn't immediately over me, I opened my heavy-lidded eyes to see him staring with raw hunger. Then he leaned forward, lifted my hips slightly, pressed against my entrance, and held there. I reached for him, and he gave me his weight.

My legs automatically wrapped around his hips, and he slid inside me. I cried out at the sharp stab of pain from penetration. He held still, waiting for me to adjust. When he jerked inside, the pain was gone, and in its place, pleasure. I gasped, lifting my hips, searching, as my nails dug into his shoulders. He flexed inside me, and a wave of need flooded me.

As he moved his hips, thrusting deep into me, every nerve ending became hyperaware. I squirmed, frantic, as he ground against my clit. My mind was a haze of lust. Time held no meaning as he played my body like an instrument, knowing how and where to touch to make my toes curl, and my breath fell from my lips in jerky puffs.

When his hand trailed down my stomach and between our writhing bodies, my eyes fluttered open to find his mercurial ones boring into mine.

"Come for me, surfer girl."

Then his thumb brushed my clit, and I exploded around him. He thrust harder, faster, and impossibly deeper until he was right there with me, falling over the edge. More of his weight covered my limp body. His forehead dropped against mine before he caressed my lips with a tender kiss. Another second, then he rolled off me, lying motionless beside me. I shivered, missing the feel of him over and inside me. It was foreign but a sensation I knew I would never get enough of.

When he stood, his boxer briefs in hand, I lifted onto an elbow to watch. Covering up that body was a crime. I wanted more. There was so much I hadn't tried since he'd controlled everything about what we'd just done. Then he grabbed his jeans, and I realized he hadn't made eye contact with me.

"Hey." I reached for him, but he shifted, and my fingers fell away. "You're leaving?" I felt vulnerable, and I hated it.

"This was a one-time thing." He bent and tossed my clothes to me. "I don't do girlfriends."

I recoiled inside, humiliated. There were no words—wait, yes, there were. "Screw you, asshole." I grabbed my shorts and angrily pulled them up. "Dating you is the last thing I want."

CHAPTER FIVE

PHOENIX

"You saw those two chicks, right?"

I dropped my backpack onto my bed in the room Shane and I shared at the football house. I loved my brother, but what I wouldn't give for my own room. As freshmen, we got what was available, and that was it.

Shane wasn't far behind, his constant prattle about girls getting on my last nerve. "I hooked up with the brunette last night. Her body was bangin'."

I didn't care. No one compared to the girl I'd been with at the cove. She'd been in my thoughts nonstop, and I couldn't exorcise our final words. As if on cue, my mind replayed it in vivid detail.

I stood and started to dress.

"Hey." She reached out to me, all soft and sexy as she lay there, tempting me to go back for round two.

I pulled away, and her fingers fell back to our makeshift blanket.

"This was a one-time thing." I tossed her clothes to her. "I don't do girlfriends."

"Screw you, asshole." She grabbed her shorts, bypassing her

bathing suit, and angrily shoved a lean, shapely leg through them. "Dating you is the last thing I want."

I pushed the images and her anger away, refocusing on my brother's attempt to engage me with a mindless lay. He'd been doing what I did when I slept with girls—one and done. I never hit it twice. Or rarely. Girls had expectations attached to repeat hookups, and I was not interested in a relationship. Shane had been a one-woman type of guy, but that had all changed after Tracey dumped him over text.

"I'm meeting up with her again after practice." He pulled his shirt over his head, tossed it into the hamper, then grabbed one on his bed, bringing it to his nose for a sniff test before putting it on.

His sling went next, and he adjusted it until his arm was positioned where it should be. Not much longer before he would be doing full practices and, if no problems arose, playing in the next game, which was scheduled for two weekends from the coming one.

"Her friend is interested. You should come with me, and I'll introduce you."

"Seriously, bro. Knock it off. I've got enough going on between classes and practice. I don't need any distractions, and chicks are the last thing I have time for." School was harder for me than Shane, and since we were in different classes, we couldn't share homework. "I told you. I'll hook up with someone during Christmas break, not sooner."

"What's your problem?" Shane shoved my shoulder.

"You know what my problem is. These classes are kicking my ass." I got in his face. Violence I could barely keep leashed shimmered around me. "Back off about women."

Something thudded, and I broke eye contact with my twin to see who thought it would be a good idea to interrupt. Cole's hand was still flush against the door, Damon on his heels. It was our cousins. I shouldn't have been surprised.

"Whatever's going on with you two, save it for the field. We have to leave early for practice." Cole walked out, not bothering to see if we followed.

Damon leaned against the doorjamb, looking like he wanted some popcorn to go with the show. I stepped away from my brother, the urge to hit him dissipating. Too many things weighed me down. No matter what, I would not screw up my chances with football.

"Why're you waiting?" Shane snapped at Damon.

"Chill, man." Damon grinned. The fucker loved watching us bicker. "Thought we could walk over together. Maybe plan how we'll continue with our fights."

I closed my eyes, imagining how it would feel to slam my fist into a nameless opponent. I needed that, but it was a considerable risk. "If we get caught, we can kiss our scholarships and football careers goodbye."

"We won't get caught. When have we ever?" Shane pounded my back as he exited the room, following Damon.

We left the house, heading for the stadium, and I fell into step with them.

The need to get into the ring outweighed my common sense. If I planned to restrict myself from girls, I sure as shit wouldn't give up brawling. Besides, it would be one fight, and I needed to take the edge off the constant worry that had been dogging me lately. "I'm in."

"I'll contact Snake." Damon jogged forward and caught up to his brother, Cole.

Snake set up the fights for us and managed the bets. We knew him from high school, and he was a rough linebacker whose nickname matched his personality.

I could use an influx of cash anyway. While our scholarship covered our tuition, Shane and I had to pay for our room and board. Mom chipped in what she could for books but didn't make enough to help past the bills at home. And I wouldn't go to our grandparents.

Besides, Shane and I had plenty saved up from fights and the excess that our cousins had dumped into our accounts, despite our protests. But I was paranoid that something would happen, and I would need more money than I had in the bank. We had very little time, and I couldn't get a job and pass my classes to stay enrolled and eligible to play. It was my shot to the NFL, and I wouldn't fuck it up.

We crossed campus as students exited the buildings where their classes were held. People stopped and stared here and there. Shane ate it up. Not Damon—he was devoted to Skylar after a strange turn of events last year. Damon had been as bad as I was, running through girls nonstop and balking at even a hint about a relationship. But Skylar had changed everything for him. I liked her. And it was his life, not mine.

Only one girl I'd met had that sort of power over me, and I was determined to stay far away from her. Just the thought seemed to conjure the real Aspen—long, wavy blond hair threaded with sun-bleached platinum strands and ocean-blue-green eyes that held secrets I longed to uncover. Her body was lean and toned with curves in all the right places. Her unapologetically wild and carefree surfer-girl vibe inexplicably drew me to her. I kept my gaze straight ahead, forcing myself not to acknowledge her. I'd spotted her on campus once or twice before, but we hadn't talked. We really didn't know each other or hang in the same circles, which was perfect. She wasn't a clinger. *Thank God.*

I shouldn't have slept with her, but it would be a long time between getting laid, since school had started, and I'd put rules in place to keep my grades on track.

Aspen broke apart from the group of girls she was walking with, and I realized I knew them, the bitch squad from Hidden

Valley Academy—Piper, Teagan, Jessica, and thankfully, no Tracey.

"Hey, Phoenix." Aspen flashed a carefree smile. "Wait up a second."

Like a fucking siren, she left me helpless against her pull. I slowed down, mumbling something about catching up to the guys in a minute. I needed to handle her fast.

"Did you want to go for coffee or something?"

I was uneasy about how connected I felt to the girl. My need for her was insatiable, and already, I wanted to lose myself in her all over again, watch her come apart in my arms. I'd never experienced that before, and I had to get far away from her because a girl like Aspen could mean the end of everything I'd worked for.

Her ocean-and-lilies scent wrapped around me in a choke hold, and my fingers twitched to touch her soft skin. Instead, I hardened myself and shuttered my expression, gazing at her with cold disinterest—the complete opposite of what I felt. "I have plans." I didn't wait for her rebuttal but took off after the guys. I had to get to practice.

With an eye roll, she pivoted, shooting over her shoulder, "Whatever. I wasn't asking you for a date." Her voice trailed off to a whisper. "Just as a friend."

The vulnerability I glimpsed from her "just as a friend" comment stayed in the back of my mind regardless of how hard I tried to shut her out. *And what the hell is she doing hanging around with the cheerleaders?* They were a problem back in high school and would be in college, too, unless we kept them at an arm's length. I shot Shane a wary look, but he and Damon had gone ahead with Cole. *Good.*

Piper and her crew came in beautiful packaging, promising everything a guy could ever dream of, but it hid what was rotten and rabid underneath. As it was, I didn't have the best outlook on women. Mom was great, but she worked herself to the bone. And my aunt Linda—Mom's sister, who'd married Lucas Savage, the dad of our cousins Cole and Damon—had been a nightmare. Manipulative, needy, and damaged. Then there was Tracey, the bitch who'd sunk her hooks in my brother for two years then bailed when she'd heard his promising NFL career had been threatened.

Those were enough reasons to support why I didn't do girlfriends. Nothing could derail my plans, especially not Aspen, just because we had an explosive connection and the best sex I'd ever had.

Besides, she was too big of a distraction. It was bad enough that I compared every girl to her and that she haunted my dreams. The chick was like a drug I had to exercise from my system, which meant she could take away everything I'd worked so hard for. I would not take the chance. The only way I would survive school and not lose my scholarship was to stay away from women and keep my grades up so I was eligible to play. But damn, if I were going to do some surfer chick, it would be her.

CHAPTER SIX

ASPEN

*I*t's the flu. It has to be.

My fingers trembled as I clutched the counter, willing my thoughts into reality. The alternative would wreck my life. Everything I'd worked for would have to be put on hold.

The stick, the one I just peed on, sat on the counter mocking me with the little open slot. I counted down the seconds until my fate would be revealed in the middle of a disgusting public bathroom. Not how I wanted it to happen, but when the vomit threatened to come out in the middle of class, I didn't have much choice.

Cold water ran from the tap, and I splashed my face, soothing some clammy symptoms that came with puking. At least no one else was in there with me. I caught a glimpse of my reflection in the mirror. I looked like hell. Pasty and sick.

The door opened, and I almost groaned. So much for lucking out by not having an audience for my potential fuckup. I recognized the tall, thin blonde from the corner of my eye. Piper. And the one who'd gone into the stall was Tracey.

I took a deep breath and peeked at the test stick. Double lines. *Oh God.* I swayed on my feet as Piper neared.

"Aspen."

Her voice echoed through the small space and snapped me out of an almost faint. I had to stay present, figure out what those pink lines meant. *Shit.* I didn't need her showing up. The required minutes had passed, and I took a deep breath and picked up the test. *Oh God.* Two lines. Faced with the irrefutable, life-altering stick in my hand, I dropped it down with a clatter and snatched the directions. My eyes scanned them again, confirming what I'd thought it meant—*I'm pregnant.*

How did I get into this situation? Phoenix was hot as hell, and I thought I could lose myself in him, forgetting about the chaos of the last five months. It seemed I was doomed to repeat some of my parents' mistakes. But not all of them. I would not get married because of the baby. I'd had a front-row seat to that train wreck of a decision and didn't wish that on myself or my unborn kid.

None of the logical reasoning I tried mattered. Fat tears rolled down my cheeks, obscuring my vision, but not before I saw Piper emerge from the stall and look at the test. Her lips formed an O before she rested her hand on my shaking arm. I liked Piper well enough, but she was connected to people who I didn't want to find out—not before I told the one person who had to know.

She leaned in and whispered, "Do you know who the daddy is?"

What the fuck? I felt sick all over again and dropped my head into my hands. I wasn't going to tell her, even though I knew without a shadow of a doubt who the father was. I'd been a virgin before that night and hadn't slept with anyone since.

"People are going to talk."

Shifting my head to the side, I glared at her.

"Okay, not important." Tracey came out of the stall, and Piper set her purse over the test stick so her friend couldn't see. "I'll catch up with you in a minute, Trace."

That was decent of her. My judgy thoughts faded. Not for Tracey, though. She thought she was better than everyone else. I'd noticed it a few times—how she would look over my head, never actually making eye contact or speaking to me. *Whatever, bitch. I don't need people like you.*

"I'll be in the cafeteria." Tracey addressed Piper as she held open the door. "Don't take too long."

Piper waited until the door shut before turning back to me. "What are you going to do?"

I shrugged. My mind was still numb.

"There's a clinic."

A clinic? That was way too much to deal with. "I don't know yet. I'll figure it out." I snatched the stick from the counter and shoved it into my bag. "Hey…" I hesitated, pausing beside her.

A soft smile curved her mouth. "You don't need to say it. I'll keep quiet about your condition."

Fuck. It was too much. "Thanks."

I hurried out, walking blindly through the quad to my dorm. I needed to let everything settle and not make a rash decision. Sleeping on it was my best bet.

But one thing was crystal clear—I had to tell Phoenix. It didn't matter that he'd brushed me off the one time I'd tried to talk to him. Even though he'd been a total asshat, he deserved to know.

Once back at the dorm, where my roommate was absent, I pulled out my sketch pad and got to work on my latest assignment. Shutting off my mind and losing myself in the drawing that I had to finish was the best course of action. Friday night or not, I didn't plan on leaving my room. I had plenty to keep me busy as well as fruit and a granola bar I'd swiped from breakfast that would last me until the next day. Then I would face what needed to be done.

The day had already been a challenge. I'd woken to an incident of praying to the porcelain god before I managed to shower and get dressed. Then I ate breakfast, fell asleep, watched a show, and napped again. It was late afternoon. My homework was done, and I'd already paced the small space of my room too many times to count. I couldn't put it off any longer. Shoes on, I grabbed my key, shoved my phone and ID in my back pocket, and I was out the door, headed toward the football house.

The walk helped. Not my nerves. Those were engaged in a battle fought in my stomach amidst rolling nausea. But my head was clear. It didn't take long to get to the house. It was about five blocks from campus and closer to where the players practiced. They lived in a huge, old, three-story Victorian building that I was slightly jealous of. I loved the character with the wraparound porch, turrets, dormers, and decorative railings. It was a pretty yellow with white trim—not what I expected, but inviting nonetheless.

I climbed the three stairs to the porch leading to the front door, rang the bell, and waited. When no one answered, I pounded on the door, not that it was any louder, but maybe it would get someone's attention. Several minutes later—because I wasn't going anywhere—a huge guy answered. I craned my neck to meet his gaze. I shouldn't be surprised. All the footballers were giants.

"Is Phoenix here?" *Crap.* I had no idea what his last name was. But with an unusual first name, only one should be living there.

"It's Saturday." The giant grunted.

"And that means...?" I had no clue.

His brows furrowed like what I'd said was foreign. "He had a game this afternoon and a fight this evening."

"Oh." *A fight? And why does this feel like pulling teeth to get any information?*

"Can you tell me where the fight is?" I refused to leave without an answer.

The guy rattled off an address. I thanked him and walked back to the dorm and the parking lot where I'd left my car. Once behind the wheel, I punched the location he'd given me into my GPS and headed to whatever the fight was. *Why isn't any of this easy?*

By the time I arrived, the sun had gone down, and a sea of cars were parked outside the warehouse structure where the fight was supposed to be. I trailed a group of people to a side door where a bouncer collected the entrance fee. It was so strange. Reluctantly, I parted with the money I didn't have to spare.

The door opened, and a large crowd yawned in front of me.

I hesitated. "Hey." I turned to the bouncer. "Do you know where Phoenix is?"

The bouncer pointed in the general direction of the stage.

Okay, here goes. The air was dense, thick with sweat, perfume, and violence—both from the crowd and on stage. Herded inside, sandwiched between people, I followed blindly until I could break free and duck into an open pocket. I stood there, taking it all in, my heart pounding furiously in my chest. The place was packed. I shouldn't be there. I ignored the stage and wrapped my arms around my stomach, uncomfortable with the voracious hunger coming from the mob.

You can do this. I pushed through, focusing on naming five things I could see—the girl jumping up and down in front of me, the silver rings on her fingers, her boyfriend's red shirt, his dark hair, and the ring ahead of me. It calmed my anxiety enough to move another few steps. I searched the sea of faces for Phoenix. He was tall enough I should have spotted him. But I didn't, and the crowd's chant finally clued me in as to why.

My gaze swung to the stage, where a man made in the image of the gods threw one powerful punch after another, kicking ass and looking good doing it. *It can't be.* But he seemed familiar, and I shoved my way through the tightly packed people for a closer look.

That same shaggy blond hair I'd run my fingers through and his mesmerizing silver eyes that burned as if he were Thor from *Ragnarok*. Okay, I was exaggerating about the glowing eyes, but still—he rained hell impressively in the ring, and the familiarity I'd sensed shifted into shock. That was Phoenix. I couldn't believe it. As if a cord tethered us, I slipped between people in my way. An elbow here, smile and apology there, and I had a front-row view.

I leaned toward a girl jumping up and down, screaming his name. Tugging her arm, I shouted over the crowd, "How long has he been in the ring?"

"Seconds?" She shrugged. "He just got in there."

Wow. My gaze snapped back to the fight. He didn't stop. The other guy never stood a chance, and with a final punch to the jaw, his opponent's eyes rolled back in his head. He crumpled to the mat, and Phoenix was announced the winner by knockout.

He stood in the middle of the stage, his silvery gaze roving over the crowd, snagging on me for half a second, then in dismissal, he faced the crowd on the opposite side. My pulse leaped at the intensity of his godlike presence. *Holy hell.* I was not prepared to see him like that.

Phoenix didn't stay there long, and another two guys got ready to fight. Rage continued to roll off him as he exited the ring and headed down an aisle roped off for the fighters. I did a quick calculation and figured out the best way to get back there then set off to intercept him. I wasn't fast enough to head him off, but I could see the door he went through.

A few guys occupied the back hallway. I avoided eye contact

and paced in front of the door, uncaring if I looked like a deranged fangirl. Ten minutes passed. My nerves threatened to get out of control, and I was over it. We had things to discuss.

Yanking the door open, I let myself in.

43

CHAPTER SEVEN

PHOENIX

I stepped into sweatpants just as the door to the locker room burst open. After pulling them up, I grabbed my sweatshirt then glanced toward the door, expecting to see Shane since he couldn't fight with his arm still healing. But it wasn't him. It was the girl from the cove. She braced her back against the door.

The hoodie dangled from my hand, and I stood frozen, taking in every sexy inch of her. Just like the first time, she stunned me, and I felt like I'd been sucker punched by her beauty and that damn undeniable connection that sizzled between us like a live wire.

What the hell is she doing here? Not that I minded. I was fresh out of the shower, and she was looking. Besides, it'd been a while since I'd gotten laid, and I could use a good postfight poke, so long as she knew it was a one-night thing—despite having slept together before. But that would be it.

"Couldn't stay away?" I leered at her, remembering the soft feel of her skin, the way she'd moaned and writhed beneath me. I hungered for another taste.

Her face scrunched in anger, and she turned to leave. I couldn't have that. I closed the distance between us in two long strides. My palm hit the door, and it slammed shut, trapping her inside with us only inches apart.

She flattened herself against the door, her eyes wide. I didn't like how nervous she was, but one kiss, and I knew she would melt in my arms.

"Don't go."

"Can you put on some clothes?" Her voice trembled. "I was hoping to go somewhere and talk."

That defeated the purpose. Confused by her conflicting signals and surprised I was still holding the sweatshirt, I pulled it over my head. It didn't matter why that was what she wanted. I was all for whatever game she wanted to play. Undressing was part of foreplay, and the way she'd checked me out told me she was very interested. I couldn't deny how excited I was to see all of her again.

"Where do you want to go?" Back to the cove wouldn't suck, or even the football house.

She tucked a piece of hair behind her ear with shaky fingers. *Why is she so nervous?*

"I... uh. Maybe the, um..."

Her face lost some color. I didn't remember her being so jittery, but I'd been heavily buzzed when we got together at the cove. I waited, not bothering to ease her nerves as I tried to puzzle out why she was falling apart.

I backed her out of the locker room and into the hallway. I didn't ask her if she drove. I guided her through the crowd and out to the lot where I'd parked, my hand resting against her back as I ignored the people who tried to talk to me. She babbled, still in those broken sentences but quiet enough that I could barely hear her. Coffee was the one word that made sense, so I drove us to the place near campus. When I shut off the car, walked around to her side, and helped her out, she stopped short just before I opened the door to the Coffee Cabana.

"I don't want to go in." She turned to me, her expression more anxious than before.

"Okay." *What is going on with her?*

Movement caught my eye, and I looked over her shoulder at Tracey strolling arm in arm with Dominick Reynolds—a senior and MLB hopeful. The gold digger, that would annihilate Shane. Since she'd dumped him, he'd been sleeping his way through one of the sororities when he wasn't moping around. I should say something to her.

Aspen stumbled over some words, her hand tightening on my forearm. An alarm went off in some part of my brain because it sounded an awful like she said she was pregnant. *But that can't be right. It abso-fucking-lutely can't be right.*

Aspen

Phoenix wasn't taking it well. We'd moved away from the coffee shop and closer to his SUV as a couple I couldn't quite see entered the building. I leaned against the vehicle as he paced back and forth, hands tangled in his hair as he shook his head. I stiffened, waiting for his denial while my gut tensed painfully. It didn't take long.

"We were drunk."

I scowled. "Not that drunk. And booze doesn't dilute sperm."

He stopped inches from my face, his silver eyes swirling with a deadly concoction of anger and panic. "You said you were on the pill."

"What? No. I never told you that."

"You did. You said you were protected. Why the hell else wouldn't I have used a condom?"

The memory of that moment flashed through my mind, and I saw myself again, bobbing, unsteady without his support, completely naked, vulnerable. He had asked if I was protected, and to my horror, I realized that I may have nodded.

"Are you sure?"

"Listen, asshole." I pounced. "I was a virgin. I haven't been with anyone since you." I was so angry I was shaking. I wanted him to pay for making me defend myself and tossed in a dig to strike at his ego. "Besides, it wasn't good enough to make me want to give it another go."

The fucker had pissed me off. I hoped he thought he sucked in bed and that he'd ruined sex for me. At my lie, a self-assured smirk chased away the panic on his face. *Great.* That wasn't what my insult was meant to do.

He backed me against the car, and the press of his big, hard body did unwanted things to mine. *Fine.* I could admit it. I was insanely attracted to him—but just my traitorous body, not my mind. Then his hand was at my neck, and he had my complete attention as the vivid memory of our one time together exploded in my thoughts.

His fingers were firm against my skin, just like they had been then, holding me in place with my back against the car. A burst of heat ignited low in my belly, and I had to swallow the moan that threatened to escape. My pulse slammed against his thumb, betraying how much he turned me on.

"We need to get a couple of things straight here."

His deep voice vibrated through his chest and into me, weakening my knees, and the need to squirm against him was almost unbearable.

"I was asking if you're sure you're pregnant, not if it's mine."

He leaned in, his stubbled face brushing along my cheek, causing shivers to erupt over every inch of me. I couldn't move if I wanted to. My breath quickened, coming in small pants of anticipation. I fought a losing battle to control myself as he whispered in my ear.

"I knew you were a virgin. It isn't something a girl can hide."

Embarrassment flooded me, effectively dousing the lust he'd incited. I placed my hands on his chest and shoved him. He released my throat and backed up a few steps. I knew I wasn't strong enough to move him. He'd let me.

I hated that he had control and didn't seem as affected as I was. His words echoed loudly through my mind, a dark stain on my memory. *Did I do something wrong when we slept together?* I had no experience from which to draw. *Was I bad in bed? Is that why he could tell?* I hadn't bled. I'd checked. It bothered me more than I wanted to admit, which meant I definitely couldn't ask him how he could tell.

A wall seemed to slam over his features, dissipating the lust I'd glimpsed only moments ago, and I shivered from its loss. I didn't want to deal with whatever he threw at me next. *Will he deny the baby's his or say I'm a slut?*

"What do you want to do?"

My head snapped back as if he'd slapped me because I could guess what he wanted to know, and my temper reignited. "Look, I get that this is a shock. It sure as hell was to me yesterday. But all I wanted to do was tell you." I poked him in the chest. "That's it. You're off the hook. I don't want anything from you. It's my responsibility now." I said the words with conviction, punctuating each point by jabbing my finger harder, but inside, I screamed at the top of my lungs. Afraid the emotions warring within would show on my face, I whirled around and hurried away. I couldn't deal with him any longer.

My feet angrily ate up the sidewalk, putting much-needed distance between us—*but is that what I want?* In the heat of the moment, yes. As fear and worry seeped past the fading anger, I faced the truth. It wasn't. Not only that, but we were far enough from my car that I would have to call for a ride, wasting more money I didn't have to spare.

By the time I was a block away, I had to fight not to look

back at him. He hadn't come after me, which told me everything I needed to know. The realization that I would be on my own—through the pregnancy and after—was my only company on my way back to the devastating reality of my life.

49

CHAPTER EIGHT

PHOENIX

I'd lashed out, and Aspen had stormed away. *Pregnant?* She'd taken me by surprise. The noose around my neck had tightened with her news. The past blindsided me with a seismic karmic punch. I wasn't foolish enough to miss the signs that history attempted to repeat itself. My hands curled into fists.

I wasn't my father. I wouldn't abandon my child.

Neither Aspen nor I had handled that well. She'd been defensive, too, but fear had swum behind her angry oceanic eyes. We didn't even know each other. But that would change because I would insert myself in her life, whether she wanted me there or not.

She'd made it clear that she didn't expect anything from me, and most guys would be relieved to hear that. I hadn't been. It also told me what she didn't say—she was keeping the baby. I would catch up with her and tell her I planned to take responsibility for my kid.

My mind whirled with the news, with how things would change. The financial obligations scared the hell out of me. What I'd gone through as a kid only cemented what I would never do. My sperm donor father hadn't done shit to help Mom

50

or us. I was nothing like him. And I wouldn't take handouts from my mom, who worked her fingers to the bone, or my grandparents, who'd paid for everything they could all my life. Besides, the last thing I wanted was to have to go to my hard-ass grandfather and ask for help. I would handle everything, no matter what.

I would get Snake to find me more fights, tapping into the underground college arena—I knew there was one. I just had to be careful not to get caught. While a baby was a game changer, it was something I could handle. Losing my scholarship for illegal fighting and my chance for the NFL was not. I couldn't dwell on that. It would work out. I would make it happen.

Decision made, I moved to go after Aspen, but before I could, an identical SUV pulled up behind mine. Shane jumped out, rounding the vehicle until he was in front of me.

I cast a lingering glance down the sidewalk. Aspen was already a block away, the streetlights casting a soft glow on her blond head as the darkness tried to swallow her from sight. That wouldn't happen—she shone brighter than any girl I'd ever met. But if my brother was there, I couldn't leave because of another potential disaster. I would track Aspen down later.

With the next problem in mind, I sidestepped Shane to block him from seeing into the coffee shop. "How'd you know I was here?"

Shane held up his phone. "Tracked you. What's going on? You left the fight with the chick from the cove. Cole saw you leaving and said you looked intense."

I rubbed the back of my neck, needing to share my burden. "She's pregnant."

"Fuck." Shane frowned, his eyes piercing into me and silently speaking in only the way my twin could.

I responded before he could vocalize his question. "That was my first thought too. She was a virgin."

"Okay, yeah. It's your kid."

I knew what he was thinking. Everybody thought I was headed to the NFL. Thane had talked me up as their secret weapon. And my record as a quarterback was well-known.

"Are you positive this chick isn't trying to trap you as a meal ticket, even if it's your kid?"

"I'm not our father." Anger raced along my spine, vibrating through me and urging me to strike out.

"No, you're not." Shane ran his hand over his face. "Just, fuck. A kid?"

"I know, man. It's a lot to take in, but I've got to step up. I refuse to be him."

"It'll work out. If anyone can manage a kid, football, and the draft, it's you."

School. He hadn't mentioned that huge concern. Adding fights could be done, but finding time for homework and studying was a recipe for disaster. Shane grabbed me and pulled me in for a one-armed hug then pounded me on the back.

"We got this."

I knew I could count on him—and our cousins, when I told them.

"What the fuck!" Shane roared in my ear, and I jerked back a step.

Oh no—*Tracey*. I'd forgotten I was blocking the window to the coffee shop for a reason. He raced around me before I could grab him, bursting into the place. Half a step behind him, I caught his arm sling, but he whipped it over his head.

Tracey's eyes went wide as he bore down on them.

"Shane, no!" I'd seen my brother angry many times before, and nothing good would come from the confrontation. I had to stop him.

Before I could, he had Dominick out of the chair, fisting his shirt. Shane's elbow went back, then his fist flew into Dom's face with a sickening thud. I lunged forward, grabbing Shane's arm as he cocked it back to rain punches on Dom.

As I dragged him back, he yelled at Tracey. Furious, Shane was a live wire, and he turned on me, hands slamming into my chest, then he shoved hard. I flew back, hitting something solid, and I reached back to shove off it. The smooth surface gave way with a splintering sound, and my hand went through. I felt nothing at first, intent on pushing off and going after my out-of-control brother again. Then someone screamed, pointing to my arm.

Shane froze. His rage fizzled before my eyes. A moment ago, nothing would have stopped him aside from me dragging him out. The pain hit in the pause where my brother looked from me to whatever I'd broken.

I glanced down at the glass strewn everywhere. My hand had gone through the display case. I couldn't even tell where I'd been cut because of all the blood. Black dots peppered the edges of my vision, and I swayed as I pulled my arm free.

People were shouting. Someone was crying. Then my brother wrapped a towel from the barista around my hand. I lifted my arm, cradling it against my chest, knowing I had to keep it high to slow the bleeding.

Shane ushered me out the door, ignoring the manager, who yelled at us about an ambulance, or maybe it was the police.

"I'm taking you to the hospital." Shane helped me into his passenger seat.

My mind whirled with what had just happened.

"Fucking Tracey," Shane cursed as he pulled onto the street and floored it.

I wanted to blame the bloodsucker ex for my sliced-up hand, but it was Shane who'd gone off the deep end. *When he discovers my part in their breakup, will he think we're even?*

My entire left hand was numb. Then there was my right one —my throwing arm—still gripping Shane's discarded sling. Blood colored that too. I kept clinging to the sling, afraid to see if I was more damaged, enough to end my career before it had even begun.

CHAPTER NINE

ASPEN

Water lapped around my surfboard as I lightly kicked my feet, waiting to catch a decent wave to ride in. After an hour in the water, I was already tired. Being pregnant sucked. All I wanted to do was sleep, but I couldn't. I had classes, assignments, studying, drawing, and the recent waitressing job because, as soon as I'd told my diving coach, I'd lost my scholarship.

Things had gone from bad to worse. While my coach had been reasonable, ensuring he would hold my scholarship for me next year, he couldn't do anything about this one. His hands were tied. So were mine.

I would have to move out of the dorms midyear—at the semester's end. I couldn't afford it. I hoped to find a place with dirt-cheap rent, even if I had to endure a few too many roommates. The meal plan would be gone too. *I can survive on ramen noodles, but could the baby?* My waitressing job came with one meal per shift, and I planned to take full advantage.

Then there was Phoenix. It'd been a week since I told him about the baby, and he and his bandaged hand had been everywhere. He was redshirting the season. None of the school's articles or the places I'd sourced on the internet had details on what had happened or how long he would be out. I wanted to know how he'd cut his hand. When I left him standing there like the asshole he was, he'd been fine. And when I asked, he said it was an accident and changed the subject.

A California gull cried overhead, reminding me of what I was doing. Scanning the water, I chose a wave and paddled toward the shore, working on picking up speed. As soon as the wave neared, I dug my arms in harder, gripped the sides of the pink-and-silver board, popped to my feet, and dropped down the vertical wall of aqua water to ride the face. I maintained my balance with one foot in front of the other and my arms extended. Worry over getting hammered evaporated from my thoughts during the smooth ride.

My heart thundered in my ears as my speed increased. Moments like that were what I lived for, and I was grateful I could continue them.

In the pocket, the wave broke behind me. White water frothed, and I kept my focus on the curl's opening. I hunched low and cut through the barrel. The wave collapsed behind me, sending a spray of water to kiss the back of my calves. I coasted toward the shore, riding out the gentle swell that propelled me forward.

That was when I realized I was no longer alone. Someone was watching me on the beach where the frothy waves broke along the shoreline. Not someone—Phoenix. *Dammit.*

Pulling myself onto my board, I paddled until I could stand then tucked it under my arm and waded out of the water to where he stood scowling. Wordlessly, he took the board, waiting until I took off the ankle strap. Then, with ground-eating strides, he reached my bag, bent, and picked it up before I could.

All the attention would be endearing, maybe even cute, if he were normal. But he was a steamroller. He thought I should take a multivitamin—then got me five kinds. He thought I should do pregnancy yoga—brought pamphlets. And he demanded I give up caffeine. Not that I drank caffeine anyway, but I didn't need him telling me what to do. As his recent antics ran through my head, I grew heated.

He strapped my board to the hood of my car then faced me. The lecture was coming.

I couldn't avoid it, so of course, I poked the bear. "Probably shouldn't be lifting the surfboard with that hand."

A muscle twitched along his jaw. Strike one. "My hand is fine."

"Really?" I crossed my arms over my chest. "Then why is it still bandaged? You would be playing in the next football game if it were all good, right?"

He advanced on me, but I held my ground, craning my neck to maintain eye contact. Familiar pangs of excitement at his nearness danced along my skin and fluttered in my stomach, but I refused to give in to the desire.

With his good hand, he cupped my cheek. "Let's talk about what's important here. Surfing."

I shrugged, focusing hard on his mercurial eyes, determined not to lean into his touch as I wanted, even though he was a colossal asshat. "It's not dangerous to surf so long as I don't take any unnecessary risks or stay out too long. Which I didn't do."

"And cliff diving?" He raised his brows in challenge.

"I'm not an idiot." I stepped back, and his hand fell away, giving me room to breathe. "And I don't need your help with anything. We're not in a relationship. We're not anything."

But that was a bald-faced lie. Alumni weekend was in a few days. My dad would be on campus, and despite how shitty things had gone at home over the past year, he still cared and was involved in my life.

Phoenix's expression turned stormy. "I don't want to be in a relationship, either, but we're tied together through this baby."

That was true. I leaned against the car and studied him—determined, headstrong, and the hottest guy I'd ever laid my eyes on, which was what had gotten me in trouble in the first place. But maybe he could get me out of some of the hot water I would soon be in by pretending to be my boyfriend, at least until Dad left.

It would be temporary, and what's the worst that could happen?

Continue reading the Hidden Valley Elite series with Cruel Hate.

CRUEL HATE

A COLLEGE SPORTS ROMANCE

CHAPTER ONE

PHOENIX

I stood across from Aspen in the beach's parking lot, and everything locked down hard as I tried to make sense of what she'd said. I couldn't have heard her right. "What?"

"I need you to be my fake boyfriend."

Fuck that. "I don't do relationships."

With her hands on her hips, she glanced at the pink-and-silver surfboard strapped to the roof of her car then gave me a death stare. "Hence the word 'fake.'"

"Why?" We stood about a foot apart, tension and attraction snapping between us like a live wire. It was impossible to tell because her stomach was flat, but I knew it was my baby she was carrying. *It might be a good idea to get her a new surfboard that says precisely that: baby on board.* I waited for an explanation, fascinated by the uneasy expression that crossed her beautiful face as thunderous waves crashed against the shore.

"It's alumni weekend, and my parents are coming."

Things clicked into place. "It'll be easier to tell them about the baby if they meet me first?"

She leaned against her beat-up, rusty, gold Honda Civic.

"Yeah. I'm having dinner with them tonight, and my dad will freak out."

I grinned, liking how this could work in my favor. "I'll do it so long as you take the vitamins I got for you and keep me in the loop about all things baby." Having Aspen as my fake girlfriend would help buffer me against aggressive punt bunnies. I had enough on my plate with trying to pass my classes and the healing hand injury—*thanks for that, Shane*—without dealing with the distraction of girls.

She rolled her sky-blue eyes. "Fine."

"When and where?"

A strand of Aspen's honey-blond hair fell against her cheek, and I had to stop myself from reaching out and tucking it behind her ear. She was so soft and fucking sexy as hell, but neither one of us needed the added complication of me hitting on her.

"Dylan's. The diner just off campus. 5:30."

I knew the place. It was one of the university's hangouts. "Do you want to go there together and further solidify the image that we're dating?"

"Yeah. Thanks."

We agreed to meet at her dorm then walk from there. It wasn't far. She climbed into her ancient car and drove off, and I headed to my SUV. My mom had to work at the hospital this weekend, so Shane and I weren't expecting her to come for alumni weekend. Just thinking about my twin brought another wave of stress. He was being a colossal pain in the ass lately. I wanted to talk to him about what was going on with Aspen and how I struggled to keep distance between us, but he wasn't emotionally available.

But maybe I didn't have to. It wasn't as if she could get pregnant again, and I didn't think she wanted a real relationship, either, given her emphasis on "fake." I pressed the start button, shifted into gear, then backed out of the parking spot.

The proposition of pretending to be her boyfriend so her parents could ease into the news about the baby made sense. And I had a particularly clingy couple of girls that having a girlfriend might help to shield me from—Jillian, in particular.

I needed to avoid the party scene and girls in general if I had any hope of passing my classes and doing what I was there to do —get into the NFL. It had been my lifelong dream, and I'd be damned if I let any opportunity slide through my fingers.

For the first time since Shane had shoved me while fighting his ex's date—*fucking Tracey*—and my hand went through the display case window, I felt lighter. I hadn't bartered for anything lasting with Aspen, but I was optimistic that eventually, that would change. She would have been a wanted distraction. I had the feeling that if we got to know each other better, she could make concentrating on important things seem easy.

I made it back to campus in time for my only Friday morning class, where I tried to pay attention, then went to the trainers for an evaluation and physical therapy for my hand. Redshirting several games was bad enough, but the initial scare that I'd destroyed my throwing hand had been mind-numbing. The cuts were deep, but the damage was minimal, and the ligaments and nerves were intact.

Thanks to Mom for being an ER nurse—she'd immediately made sure I had the top doctors and medicine. Several weeks had passed since the incident, and the hand was healing rapidly. Everyone was pleased with the progress. But it wasn't fast enough for me. I wanted back in the game as much as I needed my next breath.

The day flew by, and then it was time to meet Aspen. I crossed campus and parked myself against the brick wall of her dorm, waiting for her to come down. I didn't have to stand there long. The door burst open, and she rushed out in a flowing see-through top with tiny flowers and spaghetti straps over a formfitting sleeveless blue shirt. It was cute, and the low dip in the front and great cleavage shot was sexy. Tiny jean shorts and delicate sandals made up the rest of her outfit.

Her hair was down, catching in the breeze, and my fingers itched to reach out and slide through the sun-streaked strands. I imagined cupping the back of her head and leaning in to feel those lips on mine. I blinked, pushing the fantasy away. *God, what is this girl doing to me?* I took her hand instead, to keep myself in check. Even that touch made my heart kick into over-drive. It was unexpected, but at the same time, it wasn't. I felt suddenly more aware of her and ran my thumb back and forth over her soft skin on the back of her hand in an almost-uncon-scious manner. "Ready?"

"Mm-hmm." Her fingers tightened around my hand.

As I led her through campus and toward the diner, it occurred to me that I didn't know anything about the people I was about to meet. "Tell me about your family."

"Not much to tell. I have a sister that's a year younger. My parents are divorcing but living in the same house, so it's a war zone when Regan and I visit."

"What do you mean by 'visit'? Doesn't your sister live there?"

"Thankfully, not during the school year. Her boyfriend's parents are putting her up during school so she doesn't have to transfer or make the drive every day. I think it's because they know what it's like at our house through their son, Dane." She tugged on my hand, not giving me time to ask anything else about her sister, Dane, or the divorce. "Tell me about you. They may quiz us, and I would rather be prepared."

"What's to tell? You know about Shane, my twin. I've got two cousins that go here that are more like brothers to me. Damon is the same age as my brother and me, and Cole is a year older. We were raised in a single-parent household. My mom is a nurse."

"Okay, and your major? I already know you're a quarterback because it's impossible not to know that."

I snorted. "I've seen you with Piper"—one of the girls we went to high school with who had a massive crush on Cole—"and I'm sure she's told you plenty." Maybe. Piper seemed to be moving on from her obsession with my cousin. And she hadn't joined the cheer team, which had surprised us all.

"Not your major."

That was something Piper wouldn't know. Neither did I. "Undecided. What's yours?"

"Art and marketing." She shrugged. "Probably both."

"What kind of art?" A breeze stirred her hair, lifting it and the scent of strawberries and vanilla until I was drowning in it, craving to touch her. An image flashed in my mind of my hand fisted in the silky strands. It was going to be a difficult couple of hours.

"Mostly 2D. Sketching. Remember my surfboard?"

"Pink and silver?" The design had caught my eye, silver waves with birds coasting above the curl that looked like they were roaring off the board, almost three-dimensional.

She nodded. "I drew that."

"That's cool." Her surfboard was awesome. I'd thought it was a custom design, not something she did on her own. This chick was just full of surprises. I bet she could get a job designing board art at any of the surfing companies. She didn't even need the degree.

She shrugged, and I realized I was still holding her hand. *What the fuck?* I severed the connection instantly. It was dangerous for me to lose my focus. I had plans. If anyone could derail me, she could.

"I want to open my own company. Or maybe work on commission for a while. I haven't decided."

We arrived at the diner, and I opened the door for her. The bell jingled as we went through. Aspen grabbed my arm tightly as she led me to a man and woman sitting in a booth by the window. I could see the resemblance right away. I bent down to her ear as the reality of our scenario was about to unfold. "What's your last name?"

"Reid," she said from the corner of her mouth just before we were in hearing distance of her parents.

As we reached the table, I shifted Aspen to my left, curling an arm around her waist. The couple stood, and I smiled. "Mr. and Mrs. Reid, it's great to meet you."

We shook hands. They were careful as I'd offered my almost-healed-but-still-bandaged right one. It was okay, and I would play again soon. After we sat, the waitress brought menus and took our drink orders. Aspen's leg bounced under the table, and I rested my hand on her leg, out of sight of her parents.

"Call us Mark and Brittney." Her mom smiled. "And you're Phoenix? Aspen told us earlier today that you would be joining us for dinner."

I grinned to put her at ease, noting her keen observation of how close her daughter and I were sitting. "Phoenix Bennett. Aspen and I met over the summer then again when school started. We've been dating for a few weeks."

A gleam entered Mark's eyes. "I've heard a lot about you. Thane had a few write-ups about their up-and-coming star quarterback. Too bad about the hand. When are you cleared to play?"

The waitress returned with our drinks, and I handed Aspen the first water before accepting one. I waited until the server left and flexed my hand. "I'm already practicing, and I'll be in the game this weekend. But they have McAffrey in as the starting QB. I might ride the bench for a while. Especially since I'm a freshman."

"McAffrey doesn't read the field or have the accuracy you do."

Aspen and her mom were talking amongst themselves. She seemed okay, so I kept entertaining her dad. "He's a solid player. I haven't earned a spot yet. I'm not expecting to jump right in. Don't get me wrong—I would love to, but it's up to the coach."

Mark grunted. "It would be a mistake. I've seen your stats."

I knew he was talking about the article about the team's expectations and projections in the alumni journal, which had included my senior year stats. Bet they hadn't expected the injury.

I was impressed. I could get on board with a father-in-law like him. *Father-in-law? Damn, what is wrong with me.*

"Cole Savage is tearing it up out there. Two touchdowns this weekend, another for his brother, Damon, and the blocks from your brother. He's a tank, and we needed a player like him on defense. It was an edge-of-your-seat kind of game. I think that crowd spilled more than they drank, with all of the jumping to their feet and cheering."

"That's accurate." Brittney stared daggers at her husband—or ex-husband.

I couldn't remember if they were in the process of divorcing or if the papers had been finalized. I was pretty sure Aspen hadn't told me. "Cole and Damon Savage are my cousins." I steered the conversation away from whatever trainwreck was about to happen between Aspen's parents. "We grew up playing ball together."

"That's right." Mark whistled. "You've got some major talent in your family. Are you aiming for the draft?"

"That's the plan." That was the goal, and I would make it happen. The NFL had always been my end game.

The waitress brought our food, and the conversation shifted.

"Are you still surfing, Aspen?" her mom asked. "Or have you given up that dream?"

Aspen furrowed her brows. "I'm not giving anything up. I was out this morning."

"Why would you say that, Brittney? There's no reason she

has to give up surfing to get a degree. And you haven't quit on what *you* want." The last statement dripped venom.

Brittney snorted, her red lips pulling into a sneer. "You know all about giving up on things, don't you, Mark?"

Not good. I steered the conversation back to football, reengaging her dad until Aspen's leg bounced again, and I felt the shift in her. *This is it.*

"I don't want you guys to freak out." She had their attention now.

I grabbed her hand and held it, offering support.

"I'm having a baby."

No one said anything for a solid and uncomfortable minute. Then Mark and Brittney turned to face one another, and the insults flew rapidly.

"This is your fault," Brittney hissed. "It must be genetic. You ruined my life. Why not our daughter's too?"

"Bullshit. If anyone's life was ruined, it was mine." Mark's face turned an alarming shade of purplish-red. "You probably told her to do it. Why use a condom? Why not skip classes and make the idiot who gave in become a patsy to her every whim?"

The fuck? Heads turned as their voices rose. Our table was the center of attention. They seemed oblivious that we were even there with them. I eased out of the booth, tugging Aspen's hand for her to follow. We slipped away without them even noticing. Outside, we each took a deep breath.

"What the hell was that?" Because it wasn't about us.

"Ah. Welcome to my life." She scrubbed her hands over her face before walking toward campus, and I fell into step beside her. "That was tame. I knew telling them I'm pregnant would cause an argument. I'd just hoped to soften the blow with you being there. Guess that wasn't a good idea."

"Parents are just as screwed up as we are. Some of them just hide it better." Since she'd given me a window into her world, I decided to share a little about mine. "Shane and I only have our mostly easygoing mom. Our dad walked out on us when she told him she was pregnant. They'd been together long enough to buy a house. He left her that, thinking it was enough compensation. He never gave her a dime of child support."

She shook her head. "Wow. That sucks, but I wish one of my parents would have left. Living with both has been miserable since I was ten and Dad caught Mom cheating."

"Financial issues or not, there's no way I could imagine staying in that marriage. Not that I want to get married." I blew out a breath.

"I'm right there with you. My parents cured me of that. When they fought all the time, it got lonely."

"My mom's an ER nurse and works long hours. Without Shane, I don't know if I would have made it this far. Our dad abandoning us taught me a lot about what not to do. I'll never let my kid feel unwanted or lonely."

If she keeps it. But I couldn't ask. Handling that on top of everything else was more than I could shoulder.

We slowed at her dorm, and I had the oddest urge to follow her back to her room—and not just for sex. There was something there, an undeniable connection, and I didn't like it. I was in college for one reason—to get into the NFL. Not to fall for the surfer girl with sun-streaked hair and a background as painful as my own.

"Keep me in the loop." I dropped the statement and walked backward as she rolled her eyes and went inside. It should have been simple, but I felt the invisible pull of her like a rubber band, trying to snap me back to her side.

"Phoenix."

I whirled around as Damon fell into step beside me. Good. I needed the distraction. I clapped him on the shoulder. "Anything going on this weekend with your dad and Riley's mom coming?"

"They couldn't make it, which is fine by me." He glanced

back at the dorms. "What's going on with you and that chick? Shane said something…"

Damon and Cole were family, and I needed their support more than I cared to admit. The weight of what was going on with Aspen and the pressure of passing classes was almost too much. "Remember that party at the cove over the summer?"

"The one after Shane got dumped by Tracey in a text?"

Traitorous bitch. "Yeah, that one. I met a girl there."

"The one you were just with, right? I think Sky and Riley are friends with her. Met at the cove, too."

"Yeah, probably. Her name's Aspen." We stopped at the edge of the parking lot, ignoring the students parting around us, heading off campus. "We had sex, and I found out recently that she's pregnant with my kid."

"Fuck, cuz." Damon's head knocked back. "Shane didn't tell me that part. Just that you were seeing some girl. I couldn't believe it, not with how focused—and not on chicks—you wanted to be here."

I frowned as movement from the corner of my eye made me turn. *Shit, Jillian.* I couldn't shake that chick. I'd gone out with her twice, and she was already planning our wedding. Ignoring her and hoping she hadn't overheard us, I refocused on my cousin. "Nothing's changed."

A knowing look flashed through Damon's blue eyes, which only stirred my unease about what was coming. He saw the writing on the wall too. I was full of shit.

Everything's changing.

CHAPTER TWO

ASPEN

I slung my heavy backpack over one shoulder and left psych class, never so happy for a Monday morning class, meaning the weekend was over. I wanted to call my sister. Our parents were a nightmare, and she needed to hear what was going on from me—not them.

My next class wasn't for an hour. Regan was in school, but I could text her. I walked across campus to the library and sent her a message: *Mom and Dad are a nightmare. Alumni weekend. Call asap after school—before talking to them.*

"Aspen?" A model-esque girl glared as her gaze swept my body from head to toe.

The undertone of menace in how this chick said my name caused every muscle in my body to tense. She stood to my left. Long, dark hair swept into a high ponytail and makeup on point. Everything about her looked expensive and designer. My hand spasmed on the frayed strap of my secondhand backpack. *Wonder what I look like. Probably a mess.* I'd slept like the dead and turned off my alarm three times this morning, barely making it to class on time.

"Yeah?" By the look on her face, it wasn't going to be good, and I braced myself.

She pursed her full, ruby-red lips. "You don't look pregnant."

What the hell? "Excuse me?" I had to have heard her wrong. No one but Phoenix knew.

"I heard that you trapped Phoenix by getting yourself knocked up." Her gaze dropped to my stomach and remained there for an uncomfortable couple of seconds. "I don't believe it. Must be a ruse."

"Really." *Screw this chick.* "And who the hell are you?" I wasn't giving her anything. *And fuck Phoenix, too, for telling her.*

"Jillian, the one Phoenix actually wants." The brunette leaned forward. "Little piece of advice? You need to let him go. He deserves better than some trailer trash, gold-digging virgin who doesn't know enough to bring a condom to a beach party." She paused to smirk. "He's going places, and you'll only hold him back."

With that bomb, Jillian pivoted with a swoosh of her long hair, which came within an inch of smacking me in the face. I watched her go, my body shaking with anger. I couldn't believe he'd done that—the beach-party tidbit sealed the deal. Her information had come directly from Phoenix and not because she overheard us telling my parents at the diner.

The girl rounded a corner, and I forced myself to turn toward the library again. I was so mad I couldn't see straight. I went a couple more steps with my head down, not wanting to chance making eye contact with another viper like her. Probably why I smacked into a hard chest and stumbled back. Hands grabbed my shoulders and steadied me, and I blinked the world back into focus.

Phoenix. I should have known it was him. Fitting. I jerked free of his hold as a new wave of anger ripped through me.

"What's wrong?"

His deep voice was like a caress. Stupid hormones. My body

clearly disagreed with my brain, since part of me softened from his nearness, the feeling of his large hands on me, and how amazingly good-looking he was. But that was it. He was a total asshat, and I wanted nothing else to do with him. My traitorous hormones had other thoughts. *Am I sure I want sex off the table?* I wasn't ready to make that decision, partly because I feared I would give in there and then. But aside from that, I wanted nothing from him, especially since he blabbed to that bitch.

"What's wrong?" I parroted, my voice a whole octave higher. "Plenty. But let's start with how you should mind your own fucking business." I whirled around only to come to a screeching halt when his hand clamped down on my arm.

"Don't walk away from me," he said with a growl.

I glared over my shoulder. "Why? Are you telling me that no one walks away from you?" A cocky grin curved his mouth, and I got angry all over again. "Well, guess you'd better get used to it. This is college, and it's all about new experiences."

I shook off his hold, about to rush off for the second time, but my mouth wouldn't let me. Facing him, I jabbed my finger into his hard chest. "You shouldn't be telling people my personal business."

Confusion clouded his stormy eyes. "I didn't. I don't know your fucking personal business."

"And you never will." *Screw this and the rest of my classes.* I left, heading for the parking lot instead of the library. I needed to get the hell out of there.

Phoenix didn't follow. A part of me was deeply upset about that. But it showed me he didn't care and probably never would. I needed to stop wasting my time with him. *It's the baby and me.* That was my life, and I needed to get used to it.

Back in my dorm room, once the anger dissipated, I took another nap because that was all I seemed to do. Class, eat, sleep, and repeat. What I needed was to get a job. One thing at a time. I made a dash for the bathroom since I seemed to have to pee way more than normal lately. *Is that another symptom?* Couldn't be… I was only a little over three months.

It was nice that my roommate was rarely around, but it sucked, too, because I would have to give up my sweet setup in the dorms. With my diving scholarship gone, I took a long look at what I'd managed to save for my payment plan for school and reached the conclusion that I couldn't afford the meal plan and living expenses.

When my phone rang, I lunged for it, happy to push aside financial dilemmas. Regan's face, so similar to mine, filled the screen, and I swiped to answer. "Hey." Butterflies took flight in my stomach. I needed to tell her.

"Guess what happened!" Regan squealed, her excitement tangible through the screen.

I grinned and flopped onto my bed, happy to delay my news. "What?"

"First of all, it's been ah-maz-ing living here and not with Mom and Dad. And you'll never guess what happened last night. Dane gave me a promise ring!"

Wow. I was genuinely happy for her. If any two people could make it in marriage, it would be them. "Regan, that's so great. But what did his parents think? They know, right?"

Regan and Dane had been together for two years. Since we moved a few months before the summer, she would have had to change schools, but his parents had offered her a room for her senior year. She was much better off with them anyway.

She snorted, flipping her long shiny hair over her shoulder. "They love me. And his sister already tried to claim maid of honor. As if it would be anyone but you."

A sliver of alarm shot through me. "Wait. You're talking about a wedding like it's soon. You're not getting married before you graduate, are you?"

"No. I mean, I would. But we talked about waiting until we

graduate from college. Dane just wanted me to know how sure he is before we move in together next year."

I sagged against the mattress as relief coursed through me. It would be hard enough to juggle school and pregnancy. Add a wedding into the mix, and I thought I would hit obligation overload.

But Dane's family was wealthy. Everything would probably be taken care of for her, with very little required of me. His parents also had a condo in New York, where Dane and Regan planned to live while they went to college. Regan would go for fashion design and merchandizing not far from Dane's school, and she had a full ride, thanks to the Future of Fashion contest she'd won.

Why have I made such a mess of my life? I was happy for my sister and her charmed life, but I had made such a mess of mine. It was as if I was destined to repeat the mistakes of my parents. Destined to struggle. I never should have given in to Phoenix that day at the cove.

Intelligence and creativity were the only things our parents had given us that I was grateful for. Despite their fucked-up lives, they were brilliant, but they were stupid regarding love and made impulsive money decisions. I had learned more from them than my starry-eyed sister had. I didn't believe in love or marriage. And because I was having the baby, it was fortunate I was very good with money.

That thought made it more apparent than ever that I needed to get a job. I'd quit my waitressing one back home because I'd known the drive would be more than I could handle. Too much gas and a high risk of my aging car breaking down.

"Aspen. You still there?" Regan tapped her screen.

Shoot. I forgot I was on the phone. "I'm here. Just lost in my thoughts. I have something to tell you too."

"Yeah?"

I waited for my sister to again flip her blond hair over her shoulder and maybe even kick her feet onto a chair or table. And then she did it, and I laughed. I needed this connection.

"Remember that guy I told you about from the beach party at the cove this summer?" My stomach churned, and I wished I was in the same room with her. If anyone understood the gravity of what I was going to say, it would be her.

"Yeah. Super-hot. Model worthy. Perfect for our shop."

That was what I'd told her, and it made me smile to hear it. I had gushed that Phoenix would be the perfect model for our fantasy board shop. I could see him, even now, holding a board with my design, wearing surfing shorts of Regan's design. It had all felt so *possible* then. Everything felt possible then, but nothing did anymore.

"I can't wait for that." Regan sighed. "I wish there was a way to get it started early."

"Yeah, me too." I agreed, but the dream of owning a board shop seemed further away than ever. "There's a small bump in the road, though." *A baby-sized one.*

"Hey"—a thud sounded on her end, probably her feet hitting the ground from whatever she'd propped them on—"you're not bailing on me, are you? We've planned to open up a store together forever."

"No, of course not. But something happened, and it'll change things. I was thinking online store instead."

"Oh, phew. You scared me." Her wide grin returned.

"This'll really scare you." I burrowed into the crook of my elbow, hiding from her reaction and probably muffling the speaker. "I'm pregnant. The hot guy from the cove is the father."

"What the fu—"

The phone dropped on her end with a sharp clatter through the line. I closed my eyes, waiting for her to come back. But yeah, "what the fuck?" was the same reaction I was still having, and I'd known for a few weeks.

"Didn't—"

"Apparently not." I didn't need her to ask if we'd used protection. That mix-up between Phoenix and me had resulted in a life-altering mistake.

"Well, shit." There was the sound of a door shutting, and the slight background noise I'd heard earlier disappeared. I peeked at the screen to see the camera bob along with her as she moved from one room to another. "What are you going to do?"

"I'm keeping the baby." I understood the question my sister asked. It was one I'd wrestled with. But the truth was, I didn't plan on getting married. And I was old enough to take responsibility for a baby. It wouldn't be easy—far from it. If it had happened in high school, my answer would have been vastly different.

"Okay, I'm getting excited, then. I'm going to be an aunt."

I smiled, adjusting my phone so I was fully in the screen again. I knew Regan would be on my side. If only everyone was. "I told Mom and Dad."

"Over alumni weekend?" Regan laughed. "I bet I know how that went."

"Total disaster." I rolled my eyes. "They were so busy blaming each other that they forgot Phoenix and I were there, so we left."

"Whoa. You didn't tell me your baby-daddy went with you for that little shit show."

"I thought it would lessen the blow."

"I don't think anything could. Mom and Dad would see it as their lives on repeat."

Regan was right, and they had. "We told them we're together."

"Are you?"

"No. Not like that." My heart skipped a beat, and I frowned. "We're fake dating."

"But he's incredibly hot. How's that going to work?"

I have no idea.

CHAPTER THREE

PHOENIX

Today sucked. Aspen was acting crazy, and I didn't understand—I'd thought we were friends or something along those lines. And as I exited lit class, Jillian cornered me. Her cloying perfume hit me just before her hand latched onto my bicep, and irritation sprung from the contact, itching along my skin.

"I missed you at the party over the weekend." She leaned into me, pressing her breast into my arm as we walked across campus.

At one point, that would have worked. At one point, but not anymore. I had zero desire for her or any girl but Aspen, whom I wanted twenty-four, seven. Not that I would act on it.

A warm breeze made the palm fronds dance as the sun blazed overhead. "What do you want, Jillian?" I didn't bother responding to her comment about the party.

"I thought we could go somewhere later today… or maybe just your place." She lowered her long lashes, and her eyes gave a signal all their own.

"No." I stopped in my tracks and shook off her touch. "Look, we hooked up once or twice. It was fun, but it's not gonna happen again."

She pressed her red lips into a line before smoothing her features. With a flick of her hair, she stepped closer, placing her hand flat on my chest. "We're good together. I get you. I know football and how demanding your life is. I'm here to make it better. Easier."

I stepped back, and her hand fell away. "You're a beautiful girl, Jillian, but I'm not the guy for you." I didn't wait for a rebuttal but walked away and effectively evaded a few more girls on my way to my room at the football house.

The door slammed behind me, and I dumped my backpack on the floor next to my desk. Jillian was easy to push from my mind—she didn't take up any real estate in there. But Aspen… it seemed I was always thinking about her, the incredible softness of her skin, and how irresistible she was. I wanted to pull her into my arms and breathe her in. She always smelled fantastic.

I hadn't expected her to come at me like she had before. Whatever she'd been bitching about didn't make sense. It had to have been about the baby. There was no other explanation. Somehow, it had to have gotten back to her that I told Damon… or Shane.

Fucking Shane. He was a disaster lately. When Tracey dumped him—over text—it had badly shaken his confidence. For a while, our room had had a revolving door for punt bunnies on it. Then the frequency tapered off. That was when I suspected he'd hooked up with Tracey again. Serious relation-ship or not, she wasn't good for him anymore, if she ever had been.

I would have bet he ran his mouth to Tracey. I knew my brother. He pretended things were over between them, but I had a bad feeling they weren't. Or not all the way, even though he'd seen the proof of what a leech she was.

I couldn't control the situation, and that alone made me crazy. Trying to figure Aspen out? I was at a complete loss.

Thank God for football. Practice had been the only good thing about the day, especially since I'd been cleared to play this weekend. I should have been riding a high from that, but the stuff with Aspen, my brother, and the homework I needed to do were weighing me down. And while I could play this weekend, I didn't know how long that would last. My grades had tanked on my last few assignments because Shane, who'd always helped me in high school, had been nowhere to be found.

The door to our room opened, and my head snapped up as he entered, a small duffel in hand. He nodded then unzipped the bag and tossed some clothes onto his bed and some into the hamper.

"Hey."

He kept moving around the room, taking more clothes from the dresser then stuffing them into the bag, not acknowledging me at all.

"Are you going to be around later? I could use some help with studying."

He closed the bag so aggressively that the zipper made an angry zing. He threw the strap over his shoulder then went to the door, opening it but not stepping through as he turned to me. A muscle pulsed in his jaw, and he pressed his lips into a line. "Oh, you want my help. That's rich, considering."

He was mad. An uneasy feeling settled in my gut about why —we both knew he was talking about Tracey.

It didn't matter, though. I was going to make him angrier. "Where've you been? And why are you running your mouth to Tracey about my business?" I sounded like Aspen.

He stepped back into the room and slammed the door. We met in the middle, the clenched fists at his sides mirroring my own. Both of us itched to fight. I knew why I wanted to—the day had sucked. *But what is his problem? Other than that toxic bitch who's probably in his head?*

"You shut up about Tracey."

I stared into his blue eyes, noting how he clenched his fists so hard that his forearms bulged. "Ah, I see what's going on here. You've been avoiding me because you're back with her? What's the matter? Forget how she treated you during your injury, back when she thought you wouldn't have a career in the NFL? That didn't say enough about what type of disloyal bitch she is?" I chortled. "Or have you swept all that under the rug? Past is past. Because you're back and a contender and she thinks you're worth her while again?"

It was mean, and I kind of hated myself for saying it. I knew things about him that no one else did. And Tracey? She'd come along right when he'd needed her. At first, I'd thought she was good for him. But that lasted less than a hot minute before I sensed her true intentions. Shane never did believe me when I told him she was a leech. Or maybe he just didn't want to hear it because the positives in his mind outweighed her jealousy and mean-girl tendencies. She was the queen of using others to get what she wanted.

He didn't say a word for several seconds but kept clenching his jaw. "Let me make this clear for you. Tracey is none of your business."

"What the hell is that supposed to mean? If she's back in your life, of course it's my business."

Shane leaned in, an inch from my face. "Stay out of it. You've done enough."

And there was my answer. He probably knew what I'd said to Tracey. Or part of it.

The moment I'd intercepted Tracey played vividly in my mind because it had resulted in her withdrawing her claws from my brother.

"Look, he got some horrible news from the doc."

"Is he out the season?" Red infused her cheeks, and her hands curled into fists as she stepped closer. "This is all your fault."

"How's that? I'm not the one who hit him." Where did she get her logic?

"You threw him the ball when that tree trunk of a man was right there. You wanted him to get hurt so you could be the star, have all the attention from the coach, and get picked for an NFL team over him." She crossed her arms over her fake-looking tits. "I told him you would pull something like this."

She was off her rocker. When she took another step forward, I held out my hand, palm up. I couldn't let her inside, and no way was I going to address her brand of crazy. It would only get worse if I fed into it. I would have been the first to admit that winding her up could be fun as hell, but not when I wanted her to leave quickly. "The doc said Shane's pro career was over before it started. The damage to his shoulder is too extensive to be repaired."

"Ah." She took a half step back, her mouth hanging open. Seconds ticked by. "I thought he had PT. Are they sure?"

"PT for days, but it won't change things. And he's in a shit mood, but—"

A calculating gleam flashed in her baby blues, giving a glimpse into her dark soul before she whirled around, not even waiting for me to finish. A second later, she was in her car, pulling out of the driveway and onto the road. Once her car was out of sight, I let loose the laughter I'd been holding in.

I jerked back to the present and the sick feeling that Shane knew what I'd done. And knowing Tracey, she would drop that bomb when it benefited her the most. The worst part was that she obviously had her claws in him again. All the fight left me, and I hurt for my brother. "You deserve better."

"You don't get to decide that for me!" He jerked forward but stopped before making contact.

"You want to hit me? For having your back against a blood-sucker whose main interest in you is the fame and money you could bring into her life? Then go ahead. Let's fight. Because I'll have your back a hundred times over with her or any other chick who doesn't have your best interests at heart."

Shane tossed his bag on the bed. "I'm outta here."

What am I doing? "Hey, man." I squeezed the back of my neck, hating how I needed him for this. "Are you going to be around later? I have to study, and I could use some help."

"Yeah, I don't think so."

"Fine. Don't worry about it. I can handle my own shit." But I couldn't, not all of it. Panic punched me in the guts as he left as abruptly as he'd arrived. *What the hell am I going to do about classes?*

My head spun. It could have gone a lot worse. From the way he clammed up about Tracey, I was sure he knew what I'd done. I would do it all over again—tricking her into thinking Shane's shot at the NFL was over before it'd even started so she would break up with him was worth it. He'd had to face that she wanted him as a meal ticket. But he didn't handle it well at all, and the day he saw her with Dominick Reynolds, a senior and an MLB hopeful, he also pushed me into the display case that'd sliced my hand.

Goddammit. I fell into the desk chair and dropped my head into my hands. Shane had been spoiling for a fight. There was a reason he hadn't followed through, though—guilt. He'd already cost me time on the field from the hand-laceration incident. I knew that was why he'd held back. It was my one pass, not that I needed one. Fighting with Shane sucked, but if we'd gone at it, things would've been resolved a hell of a lot faster.

Instead, the fucker was going to ignore me when I needed him most. There was no avoiding it. I opened my bag and took out the book we were supposed to read for lit class. I'd put it off and had fifty pages to get through.

An hour later, it was clear that I could not handle my own shit. I gave up. It was pointless. Out of fifty, I was only on page five. It started to take forever when some of the words jumped out of order. Not only that, but when I tried to decipher them, I had trouble comprehending what I'd read. Normally, Shane would read the homework to me. It worked. I had a great memory and comprehended easily. When he did that, I could pass my classes just fine. But this year, when I needed help the most, he was MIA.

I pressed the heels of my hands to my eyes, trying to relieve the strain. Everything was falling apart. It felt like my football status was in danger because of the time I'd lost from my injury. My academic situation was in danger. I got Aspen pregnant. Money had already been tight. A kid would make it worse. If I didn't figure everything out, I was screwed.

In one swoop, I swept the books and papers from my desk to crash onto the floor. *Why am I so stupid?*

Fuck this. With a hard yank, I opened the right middle desk drawer and pulled out the football playbook. I had it memorized already. It was easy to comprehend. The symbols didn't jump around like words in a lengthy chapter did. And I could manage the text there, given that I lived and breathed the sport and was familiar with the jargon. I had been since I'd first held a football in my hand.

It was what I wanted to do with my life. It was my calling, what made me happiest.

The injury had terrified me. But there would be no lasting side effects, and the cuts had almost healed. I was lucky for my mom, who had gotten me the best care and was just a great mom overall, and I knew it. And one day, I would pay her back for all she'd done for Shane and me when we were growing up. She wouldn't want for anything when I was on a team and making the big bucks. Neither would my kid.

I flipped through the plays, pausing on a few to picture what could go wrong with them and other options I could pivot to. I couldn't wait for the weekend and my first game at Thane. The only downside was that the coach might not put me in, as McAffrey was the starting QB. *But for how long?* Coach made it seem like not long, but McAffrey could come out and put on a showstopper.

Aspen's dad had been right about one thing: he didn't have the same ability I did to read the field and alter plays on the fly. I knew it sounded cocky, but very few did. It was the one gift I'd been given, and definitely not from my bio-dad or even Grandad. Part of me felt like it could compensate for how stupid I was with reading—and the only people who knew about that were Mom and Shane. I'd sworn them to secrecy and even refused to let Mom get me help after sixth grade. It didn't matter. Nothing they tried had worked.

I shifted, and the side of my foot hit the lit book on the ground. *Goddammit.* I needed to get that done, whether or not the letters swirled around. We had a test coming up, and I had no clue what was going on in the book. Why the teacher had chosen something obscure that didn't have audio or a Cliffs Notes version was beyond me—it was a huge hindrance. If there had been audio, I would have been acing the class.

I glanced at my phone, but it showed no new messages. Earlier, when I ran into Aspen, I'd wanted to find out if her parents had calmed down and how she was doing. But then everything went to hell when she lashed out at me. I wanted to call her and apologize.

But I didn't know what I would be apologizing for, and I couldn't anyway. We weren't anything to each other except soon-to-be co-parents.

The playbook went back into the drawer, and I picked up the books and papers I'd strewn around. My phone rang. Aspen's name lit up the screen, so I answered.

"Hey, um… I'm sorry about snapping at you earlier."

Part of me settled at the sound of her voice and the fact that she wasn't mad anymore for whatever reason. If she could throw out an olive branch, so could I. Besides, I needed to talk to her. "Want to meet at the diner?"

"Yeah. I'm starving. See you there."

Good. We needed to get a few things resolved—specifically, whatever had set her off earlier.

CHAPTER FOUR

ASPEN

At seven in the evening, Dylan's, the popular off-campus diner, was packed with college kids but no Phoenix. I tried not to be annoyed. Too late. I was, and hunger won out. The hostess seated me, and I ordered food as soon as the waitress came around. *Screw waiting.*

I checked my phone for the hundredth time and was relieved to see a text, though it was from Regan and not him. She wanted to talk, but I couldn't. Not until I was back home. I replied to say as much then glanced around the diner, seeing a few too many familiar faces. Phoenix was cleared for the game this weekend, and I wondered how many were already fans. Maybe none were. Only the alums seemed to keep track of up-and-coming stars who hadn't seen any field time.

Instead, I pulled out the small sketch pad and pen I kept jammed inside my crossbody bag. Each time Phoenix and I were together, I noticed new things about the tattoos covering both of his arms. They were intricate, with a combination of tribal patterns and other designs that I guessed had hidden meanings. The shading was exceptional.

I etched the shape of a surfboard onto the paper from the

bottom left corner to the top right. Then I inked in some of his designs from memory, combining and adding details with meaning from my life. It made sense to me. The baby intertwined our lives. Why not create something beautiful to represent our converging paths?

As I sketched, the tension between my shoulders eased, and excitement took its place. This artwork was meant to be. I could feel the tangible nature of it taking shape on paper. I wished I had another board on which I could paint the finished design because it needed to be immortalized and free to ride the waves with me.

I tapped the end of the pen to my bottom lip as ideas came and went about my entrepreneurial surf business—the one I had yet to start. It could work, a specific line of custom designs for commission. I could start while in school. If I could get a website and pictures going, I could maybe find a way to support my little family of two.

I needed to accomplish a few things first. I flipped to a new page in my pad then got to work, making a list of just the few things I would need to do that were at top of mind. A website was a must. *Will I be able to do one myself or need to hire someone?* A tax ID and LLC were next. Social media like Facebook, Instagram, and possibly a newsletter, too, unless I dealt with that aspect with a news and media section on the website. I didn't know for sure, but I would have to do some research based on what the top surfboard companies did.

I wanted to rush back to my room and plan everything. Did I need Phoenix? No. He was proving unreliable. But...my parents would freak out even more if they thought I was alone. What if they tried to make me move home or got more involved in my life? Nope. That solidified everything right there. I did need him, just for a little while. It helped that he was so pretty to look at.

The waitress placed my food next to my sketch pad. The

smell of chicken and waffles jolted me out of the world I slipped into when creating. I stowed my paper and pen as the waitress left for another table.

I swallowed my first bite when the bell chimed over the door, and I glanced up to see Phoenix entering. The sight of him brought back the drama of the situation I was in, and I gritted my teeth. Damn it, I had been in a good place a moment before. I took a deep breath and let it all go. It was ridiculous. I wasn't mad at him, at least not entirely. I was angry at his ex-girlfriend or fuck buddy or whatever she was.

A grin curved his lips as he lowered his large frame into the booth where I sat. There was tension around his mouth. *Is that from me?* I assessed and dismissed the assumption a few seconds before he spoke. Couldn't have been. My outburst with him had been hours ago.

"Hey." I waved my hand over the food. "I was hungry. The waitress is over there." I caught her eye and indicated Phoenix. Of course, she came right over. Most women would have. The guy was hot.

He ordered and seemed oblivious to her suggestive smile and lingering gaze. Ignoring her, he held my hand across the table, playing with my fingers in a hypnotic way that had me melting until she got the hint and went to put his order in or whatever. I didn't care—she was gone.

That knowing smirk of his told me he'd noticed how his touch affected me. I sank my teeth into my lower lip and barely managed to stop from grinning when his gaze dropped to my lips. *Good, I'm not the only one who isn't immune.*

I pulled free of his touch, needing every brain cell to converse with him. What had happened that morning, how I'd acted, hadn't been entirely fair. "I'm sorry about earlier. I was upset because your girlfriend or ex-girlfriend or whatever basically cornered me."

He leaned back in the booth, brows furrowed. "What are you talking about? I don't have a girlfriend, past or present."

"Hmm." I took a sip of water. "Well, she's convinced she's your girlfriend. She ambushed me on the way to the library, accusing me of trapping you by getting pregnant. Did you know you're going places?" I couldn't have kept the sarcasm from my voice if I'd tried. "Apparently, you're doing that with her, and I'm trying to latch onto you and hold you back." I shrugged, trying to downplay how irritated I was by a stranger accusing me of things she shouldn't have known. "It was a very informative conversation." I knew I was failing on the calm front, but that girl was a bitch. I considered my little information delivery a public service announcement about a crazy girl. He could take it or leave it.

Those incredible eyes of his turned stormy, and his mouth pulled down at the corners. "I honestly have no idea who you're talking about. Did you get a name?"

"Jillian." I shoveled another bite into my mouth, chewing so I wouldn't tear into him about how bitchy the girl was. Him keeping that kind of company was a red flag in my book, no matter how delicious he looked or how badly I wanted to jump across the table and kiss him.

A muscle jumped along his jaw. "I'll take care of it. She's an annoying gnat and has never been—nor will she be—my girlfriend."

"She seems to think she is, though. Good luck convincing her otherwise." When he grinned, I forgot to breathe for a moment. "What?"

"We're fake dating for your family, but why not for everyone?"

I dropped my fork, needing all my concentration for this. "Why would we do that? I don't care what anyone on campus thinks."

He rested his elbows on the table and leaned forward. "If your parents think we're together, that benefits you. Right?"

"Yeah." *Where is he going with this?*

The waitress delivered his sandwich, and we waited for her to leave. He devoured half of it in two bites, took a sip of his drink, then paused. The dark gleam in Phoenix's eyes made me sit up straighter and take notice.

"If girls like Jillian find out that we're dating, it'll keep them away. Based on how Jillian is acting, it will only get worse as the season progresses. If you and I are dating, it'll help deter them."

"Fake dating."

"Of course." He chuckled. "I don't date. Not for real, anyway."

"I hardly see what I'll get out of the deal on campus, though." That wasn't necessarily true. My stomach wouldn't be flat forever. It might be helpful to have a fake boyfriend. It was fair, so I gave him a slow nod. "Okay, since you're helping me with my family." I laughed, just thinking about the two of us together and how my parents were. "There will be relationship issues."

"What do you mean, 'relationship'?" His entire body seemed to bristle. It was intimidating, and I tensed.

"I meant because my parents are fucked. Their relationship and the lack of one between your mom and dad are sure to affect ours."

He rested his elbows on the table and leaned forward. "It sounds like you've got plans to take what isn't real between us and make it into something it's not."

"You're out of your mind." *Is he for real? How did he jump to that conclusion?* I sort of understood how zealous punt bunnies could get—Jillian was a prime example. But one little comment from me, and he'd jumped to the ridiculous conclusion that I wanted more from him? *As if.*

"I meant it when I said I don't date. Don't think our fake

dating will result in a real relationship. And to be clear, I'm not marrying you or anyone else. Ever."

Asshole. "This is why I can't be in a relationship with Mr. One and Done."

His eyes narrowed, and a dangerous shift to his demeanor hung thickly in the air.

I didn't care. I had more to say. "Yeah, I've heard about you. Your little girlfriend"—I air-quoted the word "girlfriend"—"with the big mouth and even bigger boobs is the reason I know I don't want you. I'm not your type. And you sure as fuck aren't mine."

"Just because we're having a kid together doesn't mean we're in a relationship," he said in a growl.

I gripped the edge of the table hard and got a weird pain in my chest. I wasn't even going to try to evaluate that or the way my eyes stung from holding back tears. "You need to go."

"Finally, we can agree on one thing. I'm out of here." He tossed a few bills on the table to cover the food then stormed out of the diner.

I'm fine. I repeated it several times until I felt calmer, then tucked into the remainder of my food. There were a lot of weird things about being pregnant, including the roller-coaster ride of emotions and exhaustion. But I had to say, food had never tasted so good.

When I finished, I leaned back in my seat and noticed how busy the place was. The servers looked too few to handle it. I needed a job, and this was within walking distance, so I wouldn't have to pay for gas. After settling the bill, I had the server point out the manager then got an application and filled it out. He hired me on the spot and was even able to work around my schedule.

I would start after classes the next day, dinner shift. As I walked out, I felt better than I had all day.

I didn't need Phoenix. I could take care of myself and the

baby, especially since he'd proven that I couldn't count on him. I would not make a mistake like that again.

Dinner shift at the diner was busy. A rush came through, and I had five tables at once. Thankfully, our hostess staggered their seating, so the kitchen and wait staff weren't too swamped.

After refilling iced tea and water, I deposited the carafes at the bar and went to the kitchen to check on orders. Nausea hit me like a freight train, and I backed away, frantically swallowing as my mouth filled with excess saliva and the uncomfortable feeling that something was creeping up the back of my throat.

I dashed past Dylan, the owner, and to the restroom. My palms slammed into the door, and I rushed to the sink. I cranked the cold water and thrust my wrists under the spray, continuing to salivate profusely. Sweat beaded along my hairline, and it took a minute, but when I thought I could manage to bend without losing everything I'd eaten earlier, I splashed water on my face.

A soft knock sounded on the door, followed by Dylan's voice. "Everything okay, Aspen?"

"Yeah." I shut off the water and grabbed a few paper towels. Crisis averted, I opened the door to my boss leaning against the opposite wall. Great—first day and probably my last.

"I had Rita deliver your food." His gaze bounced around my pale face. "Are you sick?"

There was no avoiding this. "No. Pregnant." I wrung my hands. I needed this job. *Please don't fire me.* "It was the tuna sandwich. The smell hit me hard."

A small smile curved his kind face. "Come to my office. Let's have a chat."

Shit. With no other choice, I followed him to the small office in the back. It was about the size of a large closet with only enough room for his desk and two extra chairs pushed against the same wall. He waved to them, indicating I should have a seat, so I did.

He grabbed the chair at his desk and angled it toward me after a few clicks of his keyboard to pull up the schedule. "You've got a lot of shifts."

"I need the money," I injected hurriedly, panic sticky and hot along my clammy skin. Today was a light day because I was new. Even though I didn't need to shadow another waitress because of my prior experience, Dylan preferred to start his new hires with a shorter first shift.

"Okay. If you don't want to cut your hours, we can make adjustments and put you on hostess duty or something when you have trouble around the food."

I nodded, some of the tension easing. I did the lion's share of my homework on Sundays so that I could maintain a semi-balanced work-school schedule. "It's only the tuna that got to me." I pursed my lips, thinking. "And the fish sandwich wasn't super pleasant, either."

He chuckled. "For my wife, it was the smell of eggs."

I grinned. "I don't think that would go over well with me, either, to be honest."

He tapped his finger on the desk. "I would rather you didn't work many, if any, late shifts. I can move things around on the schedule to keep that to a minimum. And if you have large tables, the bussers will help you carry the trays out… or at any point you need help. I'll make it known that will be part of their job and to pay attention."

That would be strange, but it was a good idea. "Thanks. I'm okay right now, but it might be helpful later."

"Are you feeling up to working today, or do you need to go home and rest?"

"No, I'm fine. Really." Steely determination punctuated my response.

"If you need anything, let me know, Aspen. If I'm not here, my wife, Janet, will be. I'll fill her in tonight when I go home."

"Thank you. I appreciate you being so understanding." I could tell he was a fantastic boss, and I loved the environment.

After we wrapped up our talk, I returned to check on my tables feeling supported, which went a long way to bolster my feeling that everything would be okay somehow. If only I had the same sense where Phoenix and I were concerned.

CHAPTER FIVE

PHOENIX

After a long weightlifting session, as I dropped my towel in the bin and headed out of the locker room, my phone pinged. I pulled it out, and my mood soured to see a message from Stan, my academic advisor: *Can you come to my office? We need to talk about your progress.*

Shit. As if I didn't already know how bad it was going, I would have to go and let Stan explain it as if I was some stupid jock.

I had no choice, so ten minutes later, I sat in his front reception, staring at the generic artwork on the off-white-colored walls. My leg bounced as I waited for this guy to call me in for what was no doubt going to be the get-your-act-together meeting. Or worse. But I couldn't think that way. I had to play in the game. If he took that away from me, I would be lost. Football was my future.

The longer I waited, the angrier I got with Shane. If he would have just pulled his head out of his ass and helped me with the reading assignments, none of this would be happening.

"Phoenix Bennett?"

A middle-aged man with a salt-and-pepper goatee and bald

head held the door open to the hallway where his office was. I stood, towering over the portly man as he smiled and ushered me in.

"I've caught up on your stats the last few days. You're projected to have quite a season." He ran a hand over his shiny head. "How's your hand feeling?"

I flexed it as we entered his small office, where papers and folders cluttered every surface. *Weird. Shouldn't everything be online?* "It's fine. I'm back to practices and playing this weekend."

"Good. Good." He gestured to a seat on the opposite side of his desk. I sat, and he clicked a few times on his keyboard then let out a long breath. My gut tightened, and I braced myself for what was coming.

"I try to schedule these chats early, as soon as the first grades come in, so that I can head off any potential issues, but since I was out sick recently, you slipped through the cracks. I'm very sorry about that. But I'm back, and you're on my radar."

"Okay." *What am I supposed to say to that?*

He turned his monitor so I could see it and leveled me with a serious look. I didn't like the direction we were taking.

"Here's the bottom line. Your grades aren't where they need to be to maintain your scholarship requirements or to stay active on the team. In all three classes—English Literature, especially—your grades are low enough that you're in danger of losing financial aid and scholarships. You need to do well on the next few tests and your midterms to get them up."

Fuck. I stood from my chair and paced as much as the cluttered space allowed. Stan waited, letting me work through my emotions. Maybe he wasn't so bad. Time would tell, I guessed. But I needed him in my corner, and I had to curb the urge to lash out.

My options were limited. Even though he hadn't said anything, it was clear that Shane was furious with me for lying to Tracey this past summer and ultimately causing the viper to dump him via text. I'd done him a favor, though, and one day he would see that, but that day wasn't now, which meant he wouldn't help me as he had through high school. My cousins didn't know, so I couldn't ask them. I was damn good at hiding my learning issues.

Then there was the deal with Aspen. I needed her to be my fake girlfriend now more than ever to keep as many distractions at bay as possible. But fuck if I didn't keep screwing up with her. She brought out too many feelings, ones I'd never had with any other girl, and then there was the baby. But... we could help each other. I had to patch things up with her.

I couldn't talk to Mom—she worked too hard, and I didn't want to stress her out. I couldn't go to Grandad and admit that I'd fucked it all up. He was a hard-ass, and I would never live it down if he knew. He'd helped us a lot because being a single mom had been tough on her. But it was never without a price.

I tangled my hands in my hair and tugged. It was bad enough that I would have to tell my family about Aspen before big-mouthed Shane flapped his jaw at home. It would be the next step in payback in my brother's mind, and I had to get ahead of it. Not only that, but I had to get him to see that Tracey was spreading rumors that had gotten back to Aspen when Jillian confronted her. Maybe if he knew, he would snap out of it and return to being my brother.

I needed help. There was no other way around it.

Stan continued to sit patiently, and I had to give it to him that he probably knew how to deal with athletes. I fell back into the chair. "I need a tutor."

Stan's smile was pleasant, not condescending, and I resolved myself to what had to be done.

"Here is a list of tutors that will work around your schedule. They've helped many football players, and I'm sure you'll find a good match. If you prefer, you can go to the on-site tutoring office and meet with whoever's there."

I shook my head. It was bad enough that some stranger would figure out how stupid I was. I didn't need to broadcast it to an entire office. "Is there something they sign that says they'll keep this private?"

"If that's what you need, I'll ensure a contract is ready when you choose a tutor."

"It doesn't matter. You can pick one for me."

"All right. I'll get someone set up for tonight after practice."

"That soon?" My shoulders tensed. I thought I would have a few days to get used to working with a stranger.

"We need to get ahead of this, Phoenix. No one—and I'm sure you feel the strongest about this—wants you to lose your eligibility and financial aid. I'll send you the details in about an hour. I can have him start tomorrow if that works better for you."

"No, it's fine." *I might as well get it over with.*

The meeting concluded, I headed out and back to the football house. I left feeling only slightly better than I had going in. If I could get the tutor to read the book or find me an audio version somewhere, then I would do fine on midterms.

"Damn you, Shane." I muttered some version of that as I walked. When I got home, I had only about ten minutes until it was time to leave for practice. I stopped and asked Bryce, one of the defensive ends, if he'd seen my brother, but he hadn't. Neither had Jaxon. I stopped there because of course my brother wasn't there.

It was too much to deal with, and I wouldn't even have been in that situation if he hadn't been so determined to sleep with the entire female population as a balm to his very bruised ego when we got here. Hooking up with Tracey again had been the worst thing for him. She was the cause of his messed-up perception, even though I thought he'd finally come to terms with how she'd used him. It was fucked up. He'd blown off helping me, even knowing how much I needed him. I'd tried so fucking hard, but it didn't matter. Nothing did.

I grabbed what I needed and left, heading for my SUV then the stadium. *Maybe I should take this year off and get a full-time job. Save some money for the kid and school. It isn't like I'll get drafted my first year, anyway.*

I rounded the corner that would take me to the lot where I'd left my car. I stopped short, fixated on the blonde laughing about three feet away. *What the hell is Aspen doing?*

Her arm was threaded with one belonging to a tall guy with black hair. Their heads were bent close, and whatever he said made her laugh. I saw red. She shouldn't have been dating around.

In long strides, I ate up the distance between us, glaring at the guy the entire time. His eyes widened, and he stopped walking. Confusion settled over Aspen's features as she looked at him then followed his line of sight right to me.

"Phoenix." Aspen's mouth tightened, and she let go of the guy's arm.

"What the hell are you doing?" I jammed my index finger into the guy's chest, pushing him back a step with ease. "Aspen isn't yours. She's my girlfriend. Which means hands the fuck off of her."

"Max is a friend, Phoenix." She swatted my hand away from the guy and stepped in front of him.

She smacked me in the chest and tried to push me back. That didn't happen. She kept her hand on me, which calmed me enough not to punch the loser in the face.

Over her shoulder, she addressed the guy. "I'll catch up with you later, Max."

"You sure you'll be okay?"

I bared my teeth. Fucker was asking to get punched.

"Yeah, promise." She grabbed my arm and tugged until I followed her a few feet away.

"What the hell do you think you're doing? Max is my friend." She threw her arms up. "And who the hell are you to tell me who I can hang out with? I talked about fake dating, but I didn't order a side of psycho with that. You are the one who doesn't date, so your girlfriend comment was bullshit."

"We're fake dating."

"No. That went to hell at the diner. Nothing was established. You blew up and were a total asshole."

"You tried to make it more than fake. I told you I didn't want a relationship. Never will."

She smacked herself on the forehead, her eyes briefly closing. "Neither one of us wants a relationship. The fake dating was supposed to be a mutually beneficial arrangement, not anything real. It'll keep my parents off my back, sort of. And you wanted to keep girls away so you can keep your sight on whatever it is you need to focus on."

"And that's what we're doing."

"Ahhh. You drive me crazy."

The feeling was mutual. I crossed my arms over my chest, ready to drop some rules around our fake relationship, so we were both on the same page. "It's official, then. We're fake dating. Which means no dating anyone else."

"That goes both ways." She mirrored my posture.

I shrugged. I had no intention of dating anyone else. "I don't date, so that's not a problem."

Her eyes narrowed. "That means no sleeping around, either. If we're doing this, we're going all the way. I don't want to deal with bimbos regaling me with what they did with you the other night."

"Fine." That wouldn't be a problem. "Same goes with you."

"Yep. And then there's the baby." She waved to her stomach. "This isn't going to stay flat forever."

And just like that, I could picture her stomach swelling with our baby. A wave of possessiveness hit me hard, and I realized how excited I was. But that was not something I could unpack just then. "Let's revisit this tonight. I have to get to practice."

"Fine. My dorm, since my roommate is basically living with her boyfriend and is never there."

There were people everywhere. Some cast us curious glances, and I knew it was the perfect time to seal the deal. I hadn't forgotten our time together at the cove. It played far too often like a movie in my mind.

I moved closer to her, my hand at her hip. Another threaded into the back of her silky hair, tilting her face toward me. "Then let's make this official and public too."

I slanted my mouth over hers, reveling in the small gasp that escaped her lips as she melted into me. Her arms wound around my neck, and my heart stuttered with how right it felt to hold her. The heat of her body pressed enticingly against mine made everything around us fade into nothingness. She moaned, and I pulled her tighter in my embrace. God, I wanted all of her.

Awareness ripped through me. In my arms, she was responsive, willing, and so goddammed addictive. If I didn't pull back, I wasn't sure I would be able to stop.

CHAPTER SIX

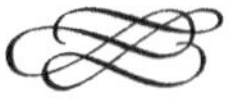

ASPEN

Phoenix was late. No text. No call. And I knew football practice had ended hours before. His lack of consideration proved that I couldn't count on him. It wasn't going to work.

"The guy's a jerk, Aspen. Do not put up with him ghosting you."

I stood in the hall with Max, my new friend from 2D design class. "No arguments here, but there are extenuating circumstances."

"Girl, no guy is worth waiting around for. Even one as hot as Phoenix fucking Bennett." Max fanned himself. "Trust me on that."

I laughed. "I agree with you on both points. And are you blushing?" I leaned closer and tapped my finger on his flushed cheek.

He rolled his eyes, and I laughed again. I was lucky to have met him, and that he lived on the floor above me was the icing on the cake. I'd caught him on the way to the gym when I was trying to storm out and go for a walk, since waiting for Phoenix was making the walls of my room close in on me.

"I may have peeked at one of the football practices when I went to watch Joel."

"Cheerleader Joel? Are you guys dating?"

"Not exactly." A slow grin pulled at his mouth, and the wicked gleam in his dark eyes told me all I needed to know. "But back to the douche canoe *you're* 'dating.'" He air-quoted. "He's a big deal to the team. And... I can see why, even though I hate the guy. He's talented."

I shrugged because I didn't care. "That has nothing to do with me."

"Doesn't it?" Max frowned. "You're supposedly dating an NFL hopeful. He's a big deal, and it's only going to get worse on campus."

"I don't care about any of that, Max. And to be honest, I don't know if it's worth continuing with this lie just to keep my parents off my back." I sucked in a breath as the prospect of being alone this year set in. Even though he was a new friend, I knew Max would be there for me as much as he could. My sister, too, but neither of them could be there for every doctor's appointment or to help with notes if I wasn't feeling like going to class. And—oh, God—the body changes. I wasn't even able to face the thought of it. I had to give up diving. I would not give up surfing.

My first doctor's appointment had come and gone. I hadn't told anyone about it, but a part of me wished Phoenix had been there with me. The doc had recommended getting a book, *What to Expect When You're Expecting*. I'd ordered it immediately, only reading through the chapter that coincided with my current month. There was no way I would skip ahead. It was too over-whelming.

"Hey." Max brushed some wetness off my cheek. "It's going to be okay. You know I'm here for everything, right?"

I peered at his concerned face, wondering if he would be there for me even if he knew the truth about the pregnancy.

"What the fuck did I tell you?"

I jerked away from Max, shocked to hear Phoenix's voice. My jaw dropped as he barreled down the hall and shoved Max back. *Oh no.* I leapt between them. Max was tall, but Phoenix still had inches and about seventy-five pounds of muscle on him. They were not an even match. I smacked my palms against his chest and leaned into him to hold him back.

"Max is a friend," I growled at Phoenix, almost gagging at the heavy scent of alcohol that wafted off him. "You have no right to treat him like that."

"Get lost, Max," Phoenix spat over my head.

"*You* get lost!" *What is his problem?* "You have no right to talk to my friend that way."

Phoenix advanced, and I stumbled back. Max's hands were on the backs of my shoulders, holding me steady as Phoenix grabbed my hips then pulled me into his arms.

"I'm not going anywhere unless I hear it from Aspen." Max's voice was just as fierce as Phoenix's.

"I'm good. Promise. I'll call you later," I said, craning my neck so he could see my face. "Phoenix and I have a few things to discuss. I'll talk to you later."

Phoenix tensed, and I pinched his side when Max touched my back before reluctantly leaving. I waited until the door to the stairwell swung closed before I tried to shove him. "Let me go."

"I don't want to let you go." He swayed slightly, his arms like steel bands around me.

Huh, now he wants to be around me? Only the threat of another guy or alcohol made him want to stick by my side. "You have to back off so I can open my room."

A second passed when he dropped his gaze to my lips, and heat engulfed me as the memory of our kiss earlier today hit me full force. Physically, I was beyond attracted to Phoenix. He finally relaxed his arms and released me. I pushed him away and whirled so my back was to him, opening my door before the hall flooded with nosey neighbors.

We were lucky. My floormates should have been in the hall, given how he'd shouted at Max. When the door shut behind me, I waved him over to one of the desk chairs and took the bed. There needed to be distance between us. That was the only way we could get through this discussion.

"You told me right after practice." I was fired up, and he would get a piece of my mind. "And *now* you show up? No explanation and no text that you'll be late? I'm not going to wait around for you, Phoenix. I've got my own life and obligations that I will not put on hold because of your inconsiderate ass."

"Something came up after practice."

I waited for more information, but his features shuttered. I couldn't tell anything about what or why. "That's not going to work. Your phone is on you. A text takes a few seconds. And if it was a girl"—I could feel my blood pressure rising—"then our deal is off."

"It wasn't a girl. I just had a meeting I had to make."

I threw my hands up. *This guy.* "That's it? You've got nothing else to say to me? Fuck it." I jumped off the bed and headed toward the door, but he stood and blocked me. "Get out and forget you even met me. We're done."

Strong hands curled around my waist, and I swayed into him, stopping myself right before impact. *No.* I crossed my arms over my chest and made sure he saw how furious I was. "I don't want my kid to go through what I've been through. And so far, you've shown me nothing but disrespect. Screw this, Phoenix. This reeks of my parents' relationship, which I do not want. I don't want to see you anymore."

"I keep screwing up with you."

He eased me back until my legs hit the edge of the bed. Then he lifted me like I weighed nothing and carefully deposited me on the mattress.

"You don't want what your parents had, and I refuse to be my dad. I'll do better with communicating, but Max needs to go."

"No." He didn't know that Max was gay, and I wasn't going to tell him. It didn't matter. He needed to see me as a person and respect my choices. "I'm upholding the no dating or sleeping around part. You have to show me respect. If you can't do that now, it's clear what you'll be like when I have this baby. If there's anything you need to know, it's that I will not let you into her or his life if that's the case."

He shoved his hands into his wavy blond hair and tugged on the strands.

I narrowed my eyes. He did that a lot when he was frustrated. Maybe he felt backed into a corner. I didn't know for sure because we weren't friends. But I would pay attention. "You were late for some reason and drinking. What's bothering you?"

"Besides the fact that I got you pregnant?"

My stomach clenched. "Yeah, besides that."

He sat on the bed, so close that the heat from his body warmed mine.

"I'm flunking out of school, and if that happens, I'll lose my shot at the NFL."

Oh, wow. From growing up in the same house as my parents, I understood missed opportunities and crushed dreams. They lived and breathed that life, only focusing on what could have been rather than all they had. It made for a depressing and unhappy way of life. No matter how much he aggravated me, I didn't wish that on Phoenix.

Something in me wanted to help him. And not because of anything more than him needing the support. "I can help. What classes are you taking this semester?"

His head tilted to the side, and his gaze pierced me, almost as if he was trying to see inside me. "That's more than my brother is willing to do lately."

Weird comment, but okay… "I'm not Shane."

He got comfortable on my bed. Hands behind his head, he stretched out, taking up most of my pillow. The bed was too small for him, and seeing him lying there gave me ideas I shouldn't have had. When that slow, sexy grin pulled at his lips, I knew I was in trouble. I scowled, in no way wanting to encourage him. I couldn't fall victim to those charms again. Look where it had already gotten me.

CHAPTER SEVEN

PHOENIX

Best dream ever. I didn't want to open my eyes because if I did, Aspen would disappear. I hadn't slept that well in... I couldn't even remember how long. But the feeling of her toned little body pressed against me and her unique strawberry-and-vanilla scent was too good to be true.

And that was what it was—a fantasy. Definitely not my reality. I wanted to make her mine, to have her in my life every day. But I couldn't. She consumed my thoughts, and I had to stay focused on football and school.

Fucking school. The tutor hadn't worked out. After we'd met and he'd talked to me like I was a dumb jock, not listening to what I needed from him, I told him to take a hike and emailed my advisor. It was a lesson in humiliation I wasn't looking to repeat. Screw the tutor. I would get it figured out somehow with Shane. He couldn't stay mad at me forever. He would eventually realize that he was better off with Tracey gone.

The shrill tone of my phone alarm blared from my pocket, and I groaned. I couldn't hide in dreams of Aspen any longer, no matter how real they seemed. I forced my eyelids open then blinked in confusion at the tiny fairy lights on the ceiling. Blond hair tickled my chin, and I inhaled Aspen's scent.

She slept sprawled across my chest, not even blinking at my alarm. I pulled my phone from my pocket and silenced it, baffled by how I had no memory of going to her dorm or anything that happened after I left the bar last night. I remembered how angry I'd been after the worthless meeting with the tutor and deciding to go to the local bar and have a drink. One turned into many, and I took a Lyft back home. Apparently not, though, because I wasn't in my room.

I took inventory. We were both fully clothed. My shoes were off and by the door. Her roommate's bed was made and possibly not slept in. So nothing had happened between us, which seemed like a missed opportunity. It wasn't as though I could get her pregnant since she already was, and there wasn't anyone else I was remotely attracted to.

Her alarm went off, and after a few beeps, she rolled with her arm, flailing precariously close to the edge of the bed. I caught her, hauling her against me.

"What?"

That woke her. I grinned as her eyes popped open. She blinked a few times.

"Morning." At the sound of my voice, things seemed to snap into place, and she reared back, scrambling off the bed. I let her, loosening my hold just enough so she wouldn't fall as she found her footing. She combed her wild, sun-kissed hair from her face and glanced down, taking inventory. *Fully clothed.* I laughed, having had the same thought.

She scowled and then gestured toward me. "You passed out, and I couldn't move you."

"Which is why you decided to climb in bed and sleep on top of me?" I eased onto my elbows, enjoying how flustered she was. Color infused her cheeks, and her eyes sparkled.

"You weigh a ton. And I had no idea if my roommate would

make an appearance, but I doubt she would be okay with me crashing in her bed." She pursed her lips. "Although she would probably be okay with you being here." Then her eyes went wide. "You need to get out of here before the rest of my floormates see you."

"What's the big deal?" I swung my legs over the side of her too-small bed, reluctant to go even though I had class.

Her head snapped back. "Seriously? Mr. Q-fucking-B football player? You don't know why it would be a problem for me if people saw you up here?"

"No." Her reaction made no sense.

"I like my privacy. That'll be gone if the other girls see you. So... get out."

Whoa. That was one reaction I'd never had from a girl before. They wanted everyone to know. I couldn't say that I appreciated that Aspen didn't. The truth was, I didn't like how she wanted to keep me a secret. It stung, but I didn't understand why. I should have been happy about it. She wasn't a clinger. *Do I want her to be?*

My head was messed up. I'd had way too much to drink the night before, and it was affecting my judgment. "What's the rush? We can go grab food at the cafeteria before class."

"Ah, no thanks."

Is she turning green? "Are you okay?"

She swiped a sleeve of saltines from her desk, crammed one into her mouth, took a sip of water, and then repeated the process. A sheen of sweat appeared over her forehead, and she inhaled several deep breaths.

What is going on with her? "Aspen. Are you sick?" I tugged her over, so she was standing between my legs. With a finger beneath her chin, I tilted her face to get a better look. Some color had returned, the green sheen fading.

"It's called morning sickness, and I get it every morning."

"Are you taking the prenatal vitamins I got you? Are you eating enough?"

She rolled her eyes then crossed her arms over her chest. "Yes, I'm taking the vitamins but with food." She wrinkled her nose at the crackers. "At breakfast, not with the crackers. Those are just to settle my stomach so I don't spend an hour puking and then miss class. Speaking of which, I need to go."

"Let's get breakfast first." *Are her clavicles sticking out more than they used to? Has she lost weight?* I didn't like it and wished I could spend more time with her. But if I was going to pass my classes, go to practice, and make enough money to keep giving her some for whatever she needed, I didn't have that opportunity.

Her sky-blue eyes softened. "Look, I'm fine. Promise. I don't have time to go to the cafeteria other than to grab some fruit and eat it on the way to class. But… maybe tonight I can come by after work and help you with your homework?"

What the hell? How did she find out about how I was failing? That was a hard pass. The last thing I needed was for Aspen to know how stupid I was. "I don't need your help."

She flinched at how harshly I'd spoken to her. I needed to leave before I said something I would regret.

I lifted Aspen to the side, stood, then left her room. The door slammed behind me, and I headed to the rear stairwell rather than cause problems for her with her floormates.

We needed to avoid each other before everything went to hell.

S weat rolled down my back, and my legs and hips burned as Coach worked the other QBs and me through speed and agility ladder drills. With a short blast as he blew through the whistle hanging from his neck, we reversed, going backward.

Two chirps, and my feet planted shoulder width apart, my arm cocked back and ready to throw the football grasped in my right hand.

"Elbows in, Bennett." Coach's expression never changed from hard-core determination.

I tucked them closer as a bead of sweat rolled down my temple. We weren't throwing yet. I wanted to.

"Too tight, McAffrey," Coach instructed. "On the shelf."

On the ladder to my right, McAffrey adjusted his arms, the ball in the correct position on the "shelf" rather than at the midline, where it had been.

"Switch." Coach shouted. "Both feet in the hole."

With each blast from his whistle, we jumped forward and back. Pocket work was challenging but necessary to help us stay protected without thought. Our head coach's work ethic was intense. His drive to mold us into the best versions of ourselves on the field made me work harder than ever. He liked to involve himself in some drills, usually led by the QB coach, and I felt the team's unity in everything he did and taught us.

He changed the drills before turning us over to the QB coach, who put us through different passes, aiming for accuracy, precision, and excellence with fewer throws rather than higher reps and average results.

Coach ran us into the ground at practice, making me regret the alcohol even more.

But I didn't regret holding Aspen all night, and thinking about it made me feel less horrible about my hangover.

We ran extra drills with the offensive and defensive lines toward the end, and we wrapped up with extra sprints when he decided we weren't working hard enough.

As I ran plays, I longed to escape to her bed and have her in my arms rather than deal with Coach's yelling about how I was underperforming with my sprints out of the pocket, the ball tucked into my chest. And when our defensive tackle got a bead on me, I slid feet first. It was complete bullshit, and we both knew it.

Could I do better? Hell yes, and I would.

So long as I don't get kicked off the team, I could deal.

I wanted to talk to Shane after practice, but my brother was nowhere to be found. Cole slammed the locker next to mine closed then leaned a shoulder against it. Damon sat to put his shoes on, but I could tell he was paying attention.

"Everything all right with you?" Cole frowned. "You don't normally drink heavily during the week unless there's a party. And there weren't any worth going to."

"I'm fine. I just had a few last night to let off steam." My cousins were basically brothers, and I didn't mistake their concern for anything but what it was. They were looking out for me. Still, I wasn't going to tell them what had been bothering me last night, and having a few drinks wouldn't blow my potential career. But there was a real possibility that it could implode sooner than I would like.

"Booze is coming out of your pores, and if you keep that shit up, it'll affect how you play." Damon stood, mirroring Cole's concerned expression.

"It's Shane." I could share a partial truth without letting them know how bad things were. "Pretty sure he found out I meddled with Tracey, and he's avoiding me."

Damon snorted. "That chick is a gold-digger."

"He'll come around," Cole said. "We could have a family meeting." His lips twitched. "In the ring."

For a long time, we had settled things with some good old-fashioned boxing, a fight club of sorts, and that was what I needed. "Yeah, that would work. He won't stay in the same room with me long enough to talk. Hasn't been sleeping at the football house, either. I think he's crashing with Tracey."

Cole grunted. "I'll—"

"You can't ask Piper." Damon cracked him in the back of his head. "Riley will string you up by the balls."

"I wasn't going to, idiot." Cole shoved him. "I'm going to pick up Riles from diving practice. Tracey's got a friend on the team. I was going to ask that girl."

Weird. "How do you know that?"

"Because Riley can't stand her. They give each other shit outside of practice, but the girl is no threat, especially on the team."

"No one can do what Riles does," Damon said. "I mean, she's an Olympic hopeful. All she has to do is mention that the other girl is a problem, and I bet the coaches would kick her off the team."

"Probably," Cole agreed. "But Riles has never been bothered by stuff like that. She finds it entertaining. You know that."

Cole's girlfriend was good people. It hadn't sat right with me when Cole had it in for her senior year, effectively freezing her out at school. We'd had a few words over it. I was glad for how everything turned out. Those two would go the distance. If they could work out, maybe things could be good for Aspen and me. I pushed the thought away. I needed to focus.

"If you've got time now"—Damon slammed his locker—"I can go to the ring with you."

"Yeah, that would be good." The three of us headed out together, separating when we got to our cars. Damon and I went to the gym off campus where we sparred, and Cole went to find Riley. The gym was a hole in the wall, but it was the perfect place to fight away from our coaches' eyes—I doubted they would agree with what we were doing.

Damon and I got our gear on and went at it. Sweat rolled off me, and with each punch, I felt my head clearing. An hour must have passed when the owner flagged us down. My body was sore by the time we stopped. He was closing early, and we needed to clear out.

I grinned at Damon after pulling off my headgear and mouthpiece. He laughed, seemingly having needed to spar as much as I had. Cole hadn't shown up, and when we went to the locker room for our bags, a glance at my phone told me why. Tracey was out with Dominick Reynolds, and he couldn't find Shane anywhere.

I checked the finder app, but Shane's phone must've been turned off, so I couldn't find his location that way. Whatever. We would have it out eventually. He didn't usually hold a grudge this long.

Outside, I was surprised by how dark it was. A cool breeze swept along the street where we were parked. But I wasn't ready to go home. The only thing waiting for me there was my failing homework.

"How's Skylar?" Damon was in a serious relationship with a chick from our high school, which surprised us all. The girl had once had a serious hate-fest when it came to athletes. Her attitude had changed, though, at least for the most part.

"Great. She was promoted to editor last week."

"I bet she loves that." Skylar was one of those super nerdy hot girls involved in current events and had the intelligence to argue politics and global policies with anyone—and win.

"We should all grab food after the game. It's been too long since we've hung out."

"Yeah, let's do that. Say hi to Sky. I'll catch you later." I got into my SUV at the same time Damon did, but he headed toward Sky's dorm, and I pulled a U-turn to go to the football house.

Life had been so much simpler when we were in high school. We ran the school—not that we weren't top-tier at Thane, but it was different, and I couldn't help but worry that my secret stupidity would come out. The tutor could run his mouth or something. I frowned. If he did, I would hunt him down and beat his ass.

It wasn't until I parked and went inside that the scent of strawberries and vanilla stopped me. Then the sight of Aspen's gorgeous face almost took me out at the knees. But it was her expression and what came out of her mouth that delivered the knockout punch.

CHAPTER EIGHT

ASPEN

"What happened?" I touched the side of Phoenix's bruised face with fingers that trembled. "What are you doing to yourself?" I didn't understand. I'd just seen him that morning, and he'd had so much to drink the night before that I didn't think he even remembered confessing to me about failing his classes. And then fighting. What an idiot.

It wasn't as if I didn't know he was involved in the underground fights, but there was something so self-destructive about his behavior that red flags were going up all over the place. I was afraid he would take me down with him when he inevitably crashed.

He jerked back from my touch, wearing that permanent scowl that I'd come to know too well. "Why are you here?"

I crossed my arms over my chest and glared, matching the look he shot Devin, the defensive lineman who'd let me in. "Fine. I came to see if you need help studying, but I'm outta here since you're back to your jackass ways."

I pushed past him and raced out the door. The fine hairs on the back of my neck stood, and I suppressed a shiver, my flight instinct intense. He was behind me. I knew it. When his hand closed around my arm, I jerked to a halt, my heart in my throat despite sensing him there already.

"I'm not stupid." He growled between clenched teeth.

We stood under one of the strategically placed sidewalk lamps throughout campus, and the only reason why I even considered walking it alone. "I've never said that."

"You're thinking it."

He loomed over me, but I wasn't afraid. Maybe I should have been, but he'd never made me feel intimidated. Not in that way. Our problems stemmed from miscommunication. "I'm not. What I think is stupid is that chip on your shoulder that'll screw you out of your pro football dream."

A curtain dropped over his face, making it hard to read his emotions, and I wanted to claw at it. I hated feeling like he'd shut me out.

"That dream's dying."

Whoa. "You're a quitter?" I took a step back, and his hand fell away. "I guess I should really think about having this baby. If you quit so easily because things are tough, then how can I count on you to hang in there and be there for our child?" Tears stung my eyes, and I whirled around before he could see them and took off toward my dorm.

It didn't take long to get there, and I was relieved that he hadn't followed... or I thought he hadn't. When I opened the door, I caught a glimpse of him not too far away. It hurt even more to know that he'd made sure I got back okay.

In the stairwell, my phone rang, and I answered it without thinking. Phoenix's voice came through like a gentle hug, and I shuddered. I stopped and leaned against the railing, pressing the phone tight to my ear. "We have to stop doing this." I was so confused. I wasn't an all-or-nothing girl, but I was a something-or-nothing one.

"I know." His voice was quiet. Calm.

I wondered if he was just outside the door. "I'm not asking

for a relationship from you. That's the last thing I need. But what terrifies me is how hot and cold you are. And I'm afraid any type of relationship with you would be the same crazy that my mom and dad have. I can't live that way, even though you would only maybe be in our baby's life sporadically."

"Open the door, Aspen."

His voice worked over me like a caress, and I squeezed my eyes shut, trying to ward off his effect. Damn him. I was going to do it too. I reluctantly hung up the phone, slipped it into my pocket, and went to the door, where only the glass separated us. He was larger than life and so incredibly handsome. But there was a storm inside him, and I feared being caught in the middle. Maybe I already was.

My emotions were all over the place. I wanted him to leave me alone but also to want to be with me, and weirdly enough, not just because of the baby. Everything was so nauseatingly push and pull. I couldn't understand myself, let alone begin to analyze how Phoenix felt.

With that last thought, I pressed on the bar, unlocking the door for him to enter. He filled the doorway, and I backed up as he prowled inside. A shiver ran down my spine, and my knees went weak. He looked at me like he was going to devour me, and I suddenly wanted precisely that.

Then his hand was at my hip, stopping me from retreat. He threaded the other through the hair at my nape, angling my head. He bent slowly, giving me time to tell him to stop, but there was no way I would. I wanted this just as badly as he seemed to.

His lips were an inch from mine, and I couldn't stop myself from saying, "You can't fix all the world's problems by kissing them away."

"These aren't the world's problems. Just ours."

I melted as his lips slanted over mine. I couldn't resist him. I was in a world of trouble.

It was just like in the movies. He swooped in, his hand on the back of my head, gently but with absolute control. My knees went weak. It was the perfect head tilt, and I clung to him, wanting so much more.

Then he pulled back, the intensity crackling between us, looking every bit as wrecked as I felt from that kiss. His hand drew forward, flat against my cheek, and I closed my eyes, reveling in his touch. Neither of us spoke. His hand fell away, and I swayed until I opened my eyes to see him turning, stepping away, leaving.

I watched him go then did the same, feeling the chasm between us and wondering how we would ever build a bridge.

I couldn't stop thinking about that mind-blowing kiss as I walked back from classes the following afternoon. My head was so far into the clouds that I literally ran into someone.

"Watch where you're going," the girl snapped.

I'd walked into Shane's ex, Tracey, and of course, she had Jillian with her. I had met both girls over the summer, just for a hot minute, and I'd known it was the bitch parade from the start.

The sidewalks were crowded with students moving from one class to the next, but the three of us were at a standstill. It was stupid. I shifted and stepped to the side to go around them. Jillian's hand shot out, and I paused.

Guess we're doing this. "Problem, Jillian?" I raised an eyebrow. "Have a come-to-Jesus-moment with Phoenix? Having to face reality that you're not dating must have been hard for you. Or maybe it was learning that he has a new girlfriend that cracked your false-reality bubble?"

Jillian crowded me, but I held my ground against the taller brunette. Her overabundant chest was way too close. "Hey, I'm sorry—I'm into guys." I glanced down in case she was dumb. She wasn't, but whatever. My insult bank was low today.

"I'm not worried, Preggo."

"Original." I smirked.

"Pretty soon, you're going to get fat. Phoenix won't stick around for that and will be right back where he really wants to be—with me." Her eyes flashed demon red. Okay, they didn't, but they could have. It was how I pictured her. "I'm every guy's fantasy," she purred.

I peeked at Tracey, who frowned at that little tidbit from Jillian.

"But not Phoenix's." I couldn't help but poke the beast. "Guess you'll have to go look for that imaginary line of guys then." I shoved around her, but she smacked her hand on my stomach. *Oh no, she didn't.* Rage rose in me. My hands fisted at my sides at the threat to the life I carried.

A whirl of dark hair eclipsed my vision, and then Jillian was off me while someone put an arm around me and pulled me back. I glanced to the left to see who it was and frowned at the pretty girl with a cute chic haircut who had her arm around me before recognition clicked. It was Cass, a good friend of Riley's, who'd shouldered Jillian away from me.

"Catty bitches." Cass snickered. "They're not focused on getting a degree. Their goal is to land a husband with the potential for fame and wealth."

Riley pressed her finger hard enough on Jillian's chest to make the brunette flinch. "Back off, or I'll talk to the athletic teams about what I witnessed you do to another girl."

Jillian smirked. "I didn't do anything."

"Really? Pushing a pregnant girl who happens to be dating the star quarterback? Yeah, that's not going to go over with any of the football guys. You'll lose your chance with all of them."

"Doubtful." Tracey looked bored. "Come on, Jillian. We have better things to do than listen to their pathetic threats."

"Heard Shane's done with you"—Cass laughed—"again."

Tracey's light skin flamed red, and she whirled and stormed off, leaving Jillian behind. Jillian's mouth dropped open, then she quickly followed.

Riley turned, a big grin on her stunning face. "That was too fun."

"Thanks, Riley." But a part of me was annoyed. I wanted a fight, and going toe-to-toe with Jillian would have helped me to let some aggression out.

"Yeah." Riley's gaze skated to Cass, who dropped her arm from holding me back. "Except something tells me you don't mean that."

I'd always liked those two. We'd met over the summer at the cove, and I'd gotten to know them a little better then, including some of Riley's rough start with Cole. They were straight shooters and obviously had each other's backs. Maybe I was in their inner circle, too, since they'd taken on my battle and made it theirs.

Riley and Cass were waiting for an answer, and the rage sizzled to a slow burn. "Too many emotions. One minute, I'm exhausted then sex-crazed, crying, or quick to anger. I can't keep up with my fluctuating moods."

They both laughed before Cass gave me a quick squeeze. "I don't envy you that, but I bet Phoenix is loving at least one part of that equation."

I rolled my eyes. "Nope. All we seem to do is fight."

Riley shrugged. "Phoenix is complicated. But he's a safe bet if you want to sleep with him. I say go for it. I know it takes two to get pregnant, but you already are. Why not enjoy the benefits of not worrying?"

"Because he drives me crazy." My face flushed. *Are we talking about me using him for sex?*

"Makes for hot sex." Cass beamed. "I vote go for it."

"And on that note"—Riley glanced at the time on her phone

—"I've got to get to class. Are you going to the game tomorrow?"

"Maybe? I should be off tomorrow." I had to work later, and one of the other waitresses had been asking around to see if somebody could take her shift tomorrow. I was so tired these days that I hadn't committed.

"If you do go, text me." Riley took another few steps back, and Cass followed. "You need to sit with us. We'll have great seats."

I agreed to let her know then turned toward the dorms. With the job, I would be able to stay this semester. I had enough to get by, barely. But I wouldn't be able to swing it next semester, not with how expensive the dorms and meal plan were.

My phone rang, and when I pulled it out of my pocket, I felt relief when my sister's name lit up the screen. "Hey, Regan."

"Hey, sis. Guess what? Dane and I are coming to the football game tomorrow. You need to go with us, and I want to see who your baby daddy is."

"He's not that great."

"Whatever. We're coming anyway."

A wave of longing hit. I missed my sister like crazy, which sealed it—I was going. I made plans with her to meet at my dorm tomorrow, and we would head over together. Maybe I would call Riley after all and see if she could get seats for my sis and her boyfriend too. It was worth a shot. I didn't think I could handle nosebleed seats, which were probably all that would be left. I'd heard the game was supposed to be sold out or near to it with the rumor that Phoenix would start. I doubted it was true because I'd also heard they had a starting quarterback already.

"Aspen?"

"Yeah?" I glanced in the direction of the deep voice way too like Phoenix's. Ahh, that was why—the gorgeous, broody guy was his brother, Shane. They looked similar but also nothing alike. Where Phoenix had blond hair, silvery blue eyes, and a lean but powerful and athletic build, Shane was the opposite. He was equally athletic but stacked with muscle, giving him a much wider span. He had dark hair and blue eyes, and I couldn't help but wonder who they took after in their family.

"Little piece of advice." Shane stayed where he was, not moving any closer to whatever bomb he planned to drop. "Don't bother with my brother, kid or not. He's not the marrying kind."

Seriously? What an asshole. I barely refrained from giving him the finger. "Good thing I'm not either."

CHAPTER NINE

PHOENIX

The roar of the crowd and the rush that only football gave me saturated every cell of my being. I lived for the game, even from the sidelines, I stood by Coach, analyzing every move on the field.

We took the field, coming off an interception, which resulted in the other team scoring. When we'd gotten the ball back, McAffrey had been sacked twice for leaving the pocket and taking too damn long to throw the ball when at least one wide receiver had been open. And we were back again, after the other team scored. The stadium's volume came in thunderous waves. They were with us and against us.

My fingers curled in anticipation as the offensive line got into position. The center snapped the ball to McAffrey. He backed up, looking, looking, looking. He hesitated too long. Tension rippled through me. The tight end was open. Downfield, Cole broke away enough to snatch the ball out of the air.

McAffrey's arm went back, his sight on Cole. I stepped a half foot forward as a defensive guard broke through our left guard. The ball tipped from McAffrey's fingertips as he was sacked. Our right tackle lunged for it.

A roar tore through the opposing team's fans, contrasting with the groan from our sideline. McAffrey was shaken. He stood with the help of the right tackle. They lined back up, and I held my breath as the center snapped the ball. McAffrey dropped back, spotted Cole and launched it, only for the ball to fall short and right into the hands of the other team's cornerback. Fortunately, the guy dropped it.

A collective boo rumbled through the audience like a well-fired weapon, chipping away what remained of McAffrey's confidence.

It was fourth down, and I cringed when the defensive line took a two-gap lineup. McAffrey would go down, again. A low chant started somewhere in the crowd, gradually building in volume until I could make it out.

"Phoenix, Phoenix, Phoenix." It both pained me and pumped me up. I wanted to be on that field.

The crowd's voice grew in strength, setting a rhythm, and before the snap, Coach called a time out. I tightened the strap on my helmet, already knowing what he would do. It was fourth and eight. We needed a first down and to get back in the game.

Coach turned and yelled, "Get in there and fix this mess."

I sprinted onto the field, replacing a dejected McAffrey as the echo of the announcer rose above the crowd's cheers. "And it's Bennett coming in after several weeks out due to a hand injury."

We didn't waste time. I called the play, and we lined up. The center snapped the ball. The familiar feeling of the laces in my right hand made me block out everything but the play. I backed up, feeling where the defenders were as I swept the field. They were hungry, coming off the QB sack and near interception.

I had less than a second, found my target, then launched the ball. Damon tore down the field, looking up at the right moment.

He plucked it from the air in a two-finger catch before

pulling it into his chest and running for another twelve yards before he was tackled.

First down. We had another four plays. We wouldn't need them. Damon had gotten us within twenty yards of the end zone. We lined up, and the center snapped the ball. Cole jetted downfield.

I threw a rocket to him. He pivoted, caught it, and curled it into his chest just as we'd practiced hundreds of times. Damon kept pace, blocking two defensive players while Cole ran into the end zone. The crowd was on their feet after that. It was pandemonium.

It was my job. My future. *I can't give this up.* Somehow, I would have to work with the new tutor my advisor had sent over.

Shane was on defense, as the coach was trying a new position for him and occasionally Damon. He and Damon were beasts. They could block all day long and also had the speed and finesse to run the ball.

After a good extra-point kick, our defense held the field, and when it was my turn to go back in, I put everything aside other than the game. Playing on the university's field was amazing. By the time we wrapped up the game with a solid win of twenty to seventeen, I felt like I could tackle anything in life.

Then I glanced to where Riley and Skylar were and spotted Aspen. My gaze locked on her, and everyone else disappeared. The forward momentum of my teammates was the only thing that made me continue walking. Her cheeks were flushed, her eyes sparkled, and she glowed. She was even more beautiful than ever before, if that was possible.

"Phoenix." A deep, rough voice cut through the intimate connection between Aspen and me, and I whipped my gaze to where the sound had come from. Not even ten feet from where the team headed to the locker room, Grandad leaned against the wall with a knowing smirk on his weathered face.

"Grandad!" The euphoria from the game carried into my voice, and I was glad that he'd made it.

"Phoenix." He slapped me on the back as I paused next to him. "Great game. I'm here to take you boys out to dinner. Tell your brother."

I agreed then headed to get showered and meet up with him, and some of the post-game thrill ebbed when I didn't immediately find Shane.

Coach walked into the locker room, and a hush settled over us as we gave him our attention.

"Today ended in victory. We win as a team, and we lose as a team. Don't focus on the bad, the missed catches, tackles, or fumbles." Coach looked in quick succession at McAffrey, Jones, Davenport, and a few others. "Brush those off and do better next time." Then he briefly glanced at me then Cole and Shane, whom I spotted behind Davenport. "Help your teammates to grow and be the best they can be. And focus on the effort we put out on that field today. That's what defines and unites us as a well-oiled team."

A deafening roar sounded as he finished, bringing with it a wave of adrenaline and comradery.

"All right, get changed and have a good night. I'll see you all at practice."

Again, I looked around for Shane, but he seemed to have disappeared. He must have slipped out after the speech. I showered, changed, and headed out to meet with Grandad, who was right where I'd left him. His steely eyes met mine, and I cast one last glance down the tunnel for my brother.

"Shane can't make it. He said he had other plans. I'll catch up with him later." Grandad answered my silent question. "It's just you and me, son."

Really, Shane? Why is he blowing off the dinner? Sooner or later, I would find out what was going on with him. I couldn't believe it was all about Tracey, especially since I'd talked to Riley, who said she'd seen Tracey with Dominick recently.

The distance between my twin and me made me feel off, cranky, like part of me was missing. I hated it. But I knew Shane, and he had to work through whatever was eating at him until we could fix the rift between us. I just hoped it happened quickly.

Ten minutes later, I settled into a center table in the dimly lit steakhouse, complete with tablecloths and waitstaff dressed in black vests and white button-down shirts with bow ties, that Granddad liked. He always expected the best and loved to be the center of attention while getting it. Such grandstanding was "a throwback to his heyday," as he liked to jokingly call his youth.

I would have been fine grabbing a burger at the diner off campus, where Aspen worked. And in light of that little fact, the steakhouse was a better idea.

After we placed our orders, he leaned back in his chair. If it had been allowed, I would have expected him to pull out one of his favored cigars. Our drinks arrived, and Grandad launched into a big speech about his days at Thane, which I often suspected was how he deflected the pain of not having Nona in his life.

"There is no greater time than playing football at Thane."

"Except with Nona." His face fell, and I instantly regretted my careless words. I remembered how full of life our grandmother had been. She'd been taken from us too early, and her death had devastated Mom. Grandad—and I sometimes questioned whether he cared about anyone more than her—had seemed lost since Nona died. He'd thrown himself into work, and his already successful company had flourished.

Our dinner arrived, and he waited to speak until the waiter was gone. A gleam entered his eyes, and I braced myself for a lengthy and emotional response that I wasn't sure I wanted to hear.

"Nona was the best thing that ever happened to me." Grandad's eyes misted, and I leaned forward. "When she died, I was… lost."

"I remember. I miss her too." But that wasn't what I wanted to understand. We were in forbidden territory. Their love had been all-consuming and deep, even with their strong personalities conflicting. From what I remembered as a young kid, they always found a way to show each other love. "Why weren't Cole and Damon around? They're your grandchildren too."

He looked up and to the left. "Our daughter, your aunt Linda, didn't have an easy life. She struggled, and we did what we thought was right then. Lucas Savage wasn't our choice for her. He didn't love her the way she would've needed."

"What do you mean, 'the way she needed'?" She'd struggled with depression. It was no secret. I'd been over at the house often enough to watch our cousins try to help her and recalled days where we never saw her because she was in bed, usually with a nurse present if Uncle Lucas was away on business.

"Linda fell into a bad crowd in high school, and we did everything we could to stop the influence of the other kids, but they left their mark. Our interventions only pushed her further away. We were devastated and did what we could to bridge the gap. Part of that was giving her more freedom when she went to college."

"What happened with her friends in high school?" This was new information that I didn't think even my cousins were aware of.

"Drugs were a part of it. Involving her in parties and situations where her confidence started to slip. But she was obsessed with one of the guys in the group, and nothing we could do helped to get her away from them. We tried everything we could think of. It nearly killed her mom. So we stepped back when it was time for college. It was what Linda wanted, and it helped heal the relationship between mother and daughter, which was all that mattered to me then." Grandad's hand shook as he reached for his water.

"But not you?"

"No. We were never able to recover. Then when she fell for Lucas Savage, we were concerned. It was the same obsessive behavior on her part, but at least there were no drugs that we could tell. Lucas was slated to go to the draft when Linda told us she was pregnant. We tried to get her to move home and set him free. She wouldn't. And because I pushed, she cut off all ties with us, not allowing us to have a relationship with our grand-children."

"What about now? Why can't you try to mend things with Cole and Damon? It's not too late." It had always bothered Shane and me. Of course, we knew there was a rift and that they weren't supposed to have anything to do with Grandad. We hadn't pushed. They had their hands full with their mom and the fights between their parents at home.

Grandad ran his hand over his face as stark pain brightened the blue in his eyes. "Lucas agreed with Linda to keep the peace and felt her decision should hold even when she passed."

Fuck. What a mess. But it wasn't my problem. Mom would have intervened if she could. "I didn't know about Uncle Lucas's shot at the NFL. He gave it up because of Aunt Linda?"

"Yes. She wouldn't have been able to handle him traveling or being the wife of a professional athlete. Lucas recognized it, and he put his unborn child before his dreams." He fell silent as the waiter approached to refill our water glasses. "That's why I'm so glad you're following your dreams. You have such talent, Phoenix. And you're doing it all on your own, not taking advantage of former paths forged by family."

"Thanks." I relaxed in my seat. What he'd told me explained so much. He always helped with anything related to football and encouraged us to follow our individual paths. It'd been easy for us because we wanted nothing to do with our dad. Dropping his name had never been an option. "At least you've got Mom and us."

"I'm fortunate to be a part of your lives. I would've done more if Cecelia had let me, but she's always been stubborn." Our food arrived, and we tucked into our steaks. "She was determined to make her way through nursing school and make it as an RN. It's an admirable trait of hers, and I couldn't be prouder. But she works too hard. I wish she'd let Nona and me help with some of the bills, aside from sports fees for you two."

"If it helps any, Mom loves what she does. I don't think she thinks of working that hard as a chore. She thrives at the hospital." It still bothered Shane and me, too, that she worked so much. I would make sure she didn't want for anything when I got an NFL contract.

"And I know how much you love what you plan to do. Keep that in mind when you're dating. If you can wait to get into a serious relationship, all the better."

I didn't share about Aspen. He would be worried, and that wasn't what I wanted for him. "Nothing is going to take my eye off my goals."

"Good. You know I want the best for you."

I nodded. Even though he could be heavy-handed sometimes, he meant well.

"Have I mentioned how impressed I am with your game today? You threw for six hundred and three yards. That's a record. I bet you already have scouts watching."

It wasn't a record, but I appreciated the sentiment and his support. If I'd thrown for over seven hundred and thirty-four yards, a record both Connor Halliday and Patrick Mahomes held, I would have broken a record for most yards thrown in a single college game.

"Coach hasn't brought it to my attention yet, but that would be great."

"May I offer a suggestion?" He picked up his whiskey and took a small sip.

"Sure." I grinned. We both knew he would, regardless of what I said.

"Finish college. You will take the NFL by storm, but anything can happen. Hopefully, you'll have a long career, but if the unforeseeable happens..." He blinked hard. "I'm not even going to give that a voice because I don't want to jinx anything. All I'm saying is you need to have a backup."

"School is..." I hated how hard it was.

"You're smart, Phoenix. Don't think of anything else. If you need help, there are tutors. I know how hard it can be to fit all the studying and homework in when you're putting a minimum of forty hours a week into football. Don't be too proud to ask."

I nodded. It wasn't quite that simple, but I didn't want to get into it.

"And there is always my company. I plan to turn it over to you and Shane someday."

"I do. I'm just not sure business is my path."

"Don't you worry about anything. I just wanted to put it out there. Focus on the NFL, but keep a backup career in mind in case you need it one day. And the family business will be there waiting too." He paused and gazed wistfully into the distance. "Nona and my time at Thane were completely different. There is no comparison. I made a name for myself that's lived on in Thane's football legacy, but the real one is in my family—in you boys. Let me tell you that I appreciate how you and Shane are making your own way and not using our family name to get by."

He was talking about how the library had a plaque commemorating the generous donations from the Bennett family, which had allowed them to add to the impressive building a few years back.

I dug into my steak. There was no use in trying to interrupt.

He could talk the entire time and would take offense if I tried. Old-school. Or something.

"I'm not getting any younger, and there will come a time when you're expected to lead the family. I know you're struggling with school. But you need to stay on the true path, the family path. There should be no distractions."

I set my fork down. *What is going on? Is he sick?* "Are you all right?"

"Of course. Never better. I'm talking about your future."

I sagged against my chair. "You had me worried for a second." I guessed I shouldn't have said that, as he looked offended. Grandad was a huge man. It was too bad he hadn't gone pro. He'd always said he could have, but Shane and I had wondered whether he hadn't been invited to the draft, if maybe he wasn't quite good enough.

"As I was saying." He paused for dramatic effect.

I missed Mom and Nona being there more than ever. They seemed to soften his sharp edges. They distracted him enough that Shane and I could escape whatever lecture he was determined to impart. Grandad expected us to do as we were told. It was how he'd been raised. He was stern and often hard-nosed. There was no escape.

"You have talent, Phoenix, enough that you'll be a top pick in the NFL. There should be no distractions. If your grandmother had lived, if she were at my side today, I never would have found the drive to expand my business to its success. She was too captivating, too distracting."

I had to stop my jaw from falling open. I respected Grandad, but sitting through his monologues was painful. What he'd just said spoke to me in ways that had me wondering if he knew about Aspen and the baby.

He kept talking, and my mind spun with the message he hammered home. He was correct. If I made it, it would be my responsibility to take care of the family, to finally make sure that Mom retired and never wanted for anything again. She worked herself to the bone to give Shane and me the life she thought we should have had, especially after our sperm donor of a father left us all high and dry, aside from the house.

We finished dinner, and Grandad dropped me back at my SUV, which was still parked at the stadium. I promised I would tell Shane he said goodbye and that we would be home soon for a family dinner.

He hadn't mentioned anything about Aspen or the baby, but I got the distinct feeling he knew. Shane probably told him.

I hated how disconnected we were. I had to get him alone so we could hash it out with either words or fists. I didn't care what or how or when... I just wanted things to go back to normal between us. We also needed to talk about what Grandad had said. There was his business to consider. I had zero desire to run it, but I wasn't opposed to hiring someone qualified to oversee everything in my absence unless it interested Shane. It would have been nice to know what my brother was thinking.

I knew he could handle what needed to be done about the company and a career in the NFL. Unlike me, Shane was smart.

I resolved to focus harder than ever. If I didn't get my grades up, I could lose everything and let Mom and Grandad down.

Grandad was right. *There can't be any distractions.*

CHAPTER TEN

ASPEN

The way Phoenix had looked at me after the football game had singed my insides. Even Regan had fanned herself. We'd gone out for pizza with Riley, Cole, Damon, and Skylar. Dane was in heaven with two of Thane's rising stars to talk with.

It was a good thing Dane had come with us, as he kept Cole and Damon occupied while Riley, Skylar, and my traitor of a sister tried to fix my lack of a love life. I couldn't figure out when being single became a bad thing.

"We're not trying to say you aren't strong enough, sis. God knows we've had to live amidst emotional warfare for most of our lives. It's just that we all saw the chemistry between you and Phoenix."

I threw my hands up. "Yeah, chemistry. I'm not even trying to deny that. But that's all there is."

Damon snorted, breaking from the conversation where Dane and Cole talked about architecture and what Dane would be doing when he graduated. "There's a lot more to Phoenix, Aspen. Keep pushing him."

They'd all been saying something similar. And maybe there

was a depth to him that I hadn't even brushed the surface of, but I couldn't see it. "He pushes me away every chance he gets. Besides, I don't want to date him. I just want him to be there for the baby and not fight with me whenever we're in the same room." I wasn't sure that was possible, and based on my upbringing, I wasn't going to put my kid through that. I exchanged glances with Regan, and the argument I knew she wanted to launch into evaporated. Instead, she squeezed my hand.

"No matter what happens with him, I'm always here for you, sis."

I squeezed her hand back before releasing it. "I know. I'm going to be fine, though." But I wouldn't be if I didn't get the business off the ground soon. She and I would need to talk about it when we were alone, which wouldn't be this trip. They were leaving after we ate.

"You're one of us now, Aspen. We're here for you too." Riley leaned into Cole's side, and his arm went around her, pulling her close.

There was an ease to how they all acted around one another that I longed for. And at that moment, I knew I needed to make more time for myself rather than sink into self-pity about my situation. Tomorrow, I would go surfing. At least once a week, I was going to do it. "Hey, Regan, can you alter one of my wetsuits so I can wear it in a few months?"

"You're still surfing?" Dane's brows rose as he stopped mid-conversation with Cole.

"Yeah, it's fine. I'm being smart about it."

"Are you going alone?" Riley asked.

"What beach are you going to?" Skylar, who'd been mostly listening, asked with a flick of her dark hair over her shoulder.

"I usually go alone and to the beach ten minutes from here."

Concern darkened several sets of eyes.

"I'll be fine. I always am."

"It's not just you anymore, sis."

"Yeah, thanks." I hated the reminder, but Regan was right. I did have to be smart about what I did. "The doc cleared me to surf so long as I don't try to tackle big waves, stay hydrated, and listen to my body."

Skylar typed furiously into her phone, then a chorus of pings sounded around the table. "There. We're in a group chat now. Just message when you're going, and one of us should be able to go with you."

"Add me in there," Regan demanded, rattling off her digits.

I didn't want to be, but I was touched that they cared enough to make sure I was okay. Then I looked closer at the string and noticed both Phoenix and Shane in the thread.

"Shane's been shit about his phone lately, and Phoenix has a lot on his mind. Don't worry about them being in the chat." Cole read me like a book.

"Fine." I didn't like it, but it *wasn't* only about me, and I needed to be smart. Besides, I would have been foolish to pass up the chance to have more than just myself to rely on if I did get into trouble—or in general. "Can we drop this topic, or any that includes Phoenix, and move on to something else?"

With a wink, Riley turned everyone's attention to Regan, asking questions about the award she had won for fashion and what her designs were like. My sister could talk about that until she was blue in the face.

The rest of dinner was fun. I didn't remember laughing so much in the last few years. Even if Phoenix and I couldn't find common ground, I hoped I could stay in touch with them because it was clear they would be the kind of friends that would last a lifetime.

On that note, I admitted to myself I needed to make more of an effort with Phoenix. He was the father of my unborn child, after all, and I couldn't deny that I was attracted to him.

When I returned to the dorm, I tossed my bag and keys on

the desk and grabbed my phone. I stretched out on the bed and called Phoenix. As the phone rang, my thoughts went on a roller-coaster ride about how insufferable he was... arrogant, aggressive, uber masculine. But even with a bruised face, he looked better than any guy I'd seen. Aside from our bickering, he was everything I wanted in a man—driven, strong, charming, protective, and tough. And I had a feeling he might be smart, too, which sweetened the deal even more.

When he answered, it took me a second to remember I'd called him. After an awkward pause, I said hello.

"Is everything all right?"

"Yeah. I was just distracted." *And forgot I was on the phone. Who does that? Me. Apparently, I do.* I rolled my eyes because I was ridiculous. "I'm going to the library tomorrow since it's Sunday and the universal day to do homework. Want to meet there? I can help you with your homework."

And... nothing. Silence stretched between us, and I refused to say anything, getting angrier by the second. I had no idea what his problem was. He was the one who'd confessed he was failing his classes. I'd seen him play football and knew he was insanely talented and would get an offer to go pro if he could stay in college long enough. But with his homework problems and refusal to accept help, I was starting to doubt it would come together for him.

"I don't need help, Aspen. Stop talking to me about classes. In fact, I think we need to take a step back."

"Are we fake breaking up?" I was joking but felt like I was spiraling into a small panic attack.

"No," he replied softly.

I could hear the amusement in his voice, even as subdued as it was. Something was eating at him, but I didn't think he would share whatever it was. I wasn't holding my breath.

"Our 'dating' has mutual benefits. As far as everyone else is concerned—"

"Except for your friends and my sister."

"Right. They're the only ones who'll know the truth about our relationship."

"Fine." It's what I'd wanted all along, or so I convinced myself. I dropped my forehead onto my hand, still cradling the phone to my ear.

"If you need anything for the baby, let me know. Otherwise, we should limit our interactions."

"Got it. Later." I hung up, fighting the urge to cry.

Why does he have this effect on me?

***

"Hey." Riley grinned as she closed the SUV's door then climbed onto the ledge to free her surfboard. "How long have you been waiting? Cass took forever."

"I heard that." The passenger door shut, and Cass rounded the front of the truck, followed by Skylar, who must've been in the backseat. "And you're both insane to want to come out this early."

"Ten in the morning is far from early." I laughed then turned to Riley. "And I haven't been waiting long. I got here five minutes ago."

Skylar wore oversized sunglasses, and her black hair was in a messy bun on top of her head. She tightly clutched a book, and a beach towel hung over her shoulder. "You two do your surfing thing. I've got a spot with some suntan lotion just waiting for me."

"I'm with her." Cass grinned as they headed through the parking lot and onto the sand.

Riley laughed. "They were up late last night, and I woke them up rather loudly."

"Evil." I waited for her to get her board down then tucked mine under my arm. "But I'm glad you guys came.

"I'm always up for anything on the water."

"Same." At least I would be again after March. I looked down at my belly, contemplating how painting might have to be the thing to satisfy me for a little while, then scanned the ocean, checking out the waves. They were decent but certainly not large swells. "We should have come super early. The waves would have been bigger."

Riley shrugged, and her long chestnut hair rippled in a wave. "Next time."

The sand was warm beneath our feet even though the sun wasn't at its highest point in the sky. But the warm rays felt amazing, and I tilted my face up to enjoy it for a few seconds. We stopped to visit Cass and Sky, who already had their towels spread out and were applying sunscreen.

"I love your surfboard. Where'd you get it?" Riley set hers in the sand and rested a hand on it as she looked closely at the silver waves with the birds coasting above the curl.

"I painted it onto an old board of mine."

"What?" Sky stopped applying lotion. "That's amazing."

"I didn't know you were an artist." Riley bent for a closer look. "Have you done any others?"

"A few… It's something I want to turn into a business." Anticipation danced over my skin, goose bumps following in its wake. "My sister is in fashion and was going to design board shorts, bikinis, and wetsuits for the shop. But since things have changed…"

"What are you, now?" Cass asked. "Three months along?"

"Yeah, a little over that. And because of how things are changing, I thought I would open the business online instead of a brick and mortar."

"I love that!" Sky got to her knees, her eyes sparkling with excitement. "How were you thinking of doing it? Have you designed a website yet? Custom or a gallery of premade painted boards that people can purchase from?"

"Both. But I need to get a website—"

"I can help with that," Sky cut in. "Either with the design or the writing or both."

"That would be amazing."

"When do you want to get started?" Cass grabbed a scarf from her bag and tied it on her head, keeping her pixie cut from blowing in her face.

"In the next week, maybe? Not live because I don't have any inventory. I need to save up and get some boards."

"Sure. Let's get a few dates and times on our schedules, and we'll knock this thing out." Sky grinned. "I'll text you a few options to check against when you know your schedule at the diner."

My body buzzed with excitement. "Perfect."

"We can help look for deals on the boards too." Riley dropped her bag onto the sand.

I took that as a cue to hit the waves. "Thanks. I would love that." We smiled before picking up our boards and taking them to the water.

We waded in and paddled out on our boards. Anticipation buzzed along my skin. Time slowed as my brain captured and cataloged everything about my surroundings, hyperaware of the danger. Surfer brain—and probably something that happened with other adrenaline-junkie athletes.

Once we were far enough out, I sat on my board and let my feet dangle off the sides as water lapped at our boards. Riley did the same. A few gulls circled not far from us, looking for their next meal. We kept an eye on the waves until a familiar buzz cracked through me.

I flattened out and dug my arms in, paddling furiously to catch the rising wave. I rose quickly, and a burst of speed sent a thrill like a ripcord through me as the wave picked me up. I popped to my feet as the wave broke and dropped down the vertical wall of water to ride the face. In the pocket, I reveled in a smooth ride without worrying about getting hammered.

My heart thundered in my ears. I lived for moments like those.

I kept my focus on the curl's opening. Whitecaps frothed as I hunched low and cut through the barrel. The wave collapsed behind me, sending a spray of water. I coasted toward the shore, riding the gentle swell that propelled me forward until I dropped back into the water, twisting to watch Riley charge out of the barrel in the distance.

We shared exhilarated grins then paddled back out to catch the next one. After about an hour, I heeded the doc's advice and went to shore to hydrate, rest, and hang with the girls before I had to head to the library.

Time went by too quickly on such a perfect morning. But hanging at the beach and riding the waves had done enough to bring a sense of calmness and creativity back into my life.

I went back to the dorms to shower and change, exhausted, exhilarated, and with a plan to launch my business with the help of Riley, Sky, and Cass.

If I hadn't had a ton of homework that I hadn't touched because of work and everyday stuff that had come up, I would have gone to one of the open studio times and gotten some preliminary sketches done. But I really needed to get some reading and notes done and figured I would join a significant portion of the student body at the library, the designated place for Sunday studying.

Still chilled from the ocean, I pulled on a pair of leggings and a fitted T-shirt. My mind wandered as I walked along Thane's brick-lined walkways, complete with historic architecture, and lush greenery.

We were closing in on October, when I would be four months pregnant. I had the perfect Halloween costume in mind, too—a prom dress with a prom queen sash—with a very natural baby bump. I laughed at the thought of going to a party dressed like that. Regan would get it. We shared a similar sense of humor.

I shot her a text saying that we needed to talk business soon. The ideas for the custom surf line were burning a hole in my head. I couldn't wait to get a website set up with Sky and start working. I would need pictures and a few prototypes, though, along with money for some great boards that I could paint.

Regan and I both planned to get at least a minor in marketing so we would know what we were doing. We needed to make sure we were set up for success with her clothing designs and my surfboards.

I jogged up the stairs to the library, my backpack smacking uncomfortably against my back. A girl held the door for me, and I smiled and nodded as I reached her.

I breezed through the door, found a quiet table on the second floor, and spread my homework out in front of me. I got to work. Statistics were a breeze, and I got that done in record time and moved on to physics. It wasn't my favorite, but there was a science requirement I had to get out of the way. The last task was for lit class, and I only had a few chapters of reading to do. I cracked the book and got to reading until the heavy thump of a bag across from me startled me out of the story enough to jerk my gaze to whoever'd had the audacity to drop their crap so loudly when they could see I was studying.

Dark hair and darker eyes met mine, and I grinned, always welcoming Max. "Decided to crack a book?"

"Vixen." He dropped onto a chair. "Joel has family in town and kicked me out of his room, so I figured I might as well get some boring work done. Imagine my surprise at seeing you here on my way out."

"You're already done?" I shoved everything except the book into my backpack. I had only one chapter left to read.

He shrugged casually. "I did what I needed to... except for that dreadful math class."

"Which one are you in?"

"It's basic. 101 or something like that. Math is my kryptonite. I can't make sense of it." He frowned. "I don't know why we need it, anyway. Our phones take care of everything, and I'll hire an accountant when I make it big."

I cracked his forearm with my book and then shoved that in my bag, too, because I knew I wouldn't be getting any more reading done with him around. "I'll help you. I'm good at math."

"Figures. You're probably one of those alien people who's good at everything."

"Hardly." I laughed. He was so dramatic, but it fed my soul. I needed something fun today, and Max always provided. "Want to get it done now?"

"God, no. I'm fading fast. Let's go to The Spot."

"I'm in." I got to my feet and gathered my stuff. We left together and made plans for me to help him with his math homework twice a week as we walked the short distance to the popular coffee shop.

The Spot was already busy when we walked in. I scanned the dining area, spied a single empty table, then rushed to it as Max stayed in line. The dark wood floors and tables paired with the subtle lighting made the ambiance classy and gave the illusion of privacy. It was a favorite among college kids and locals alike. They roasted their beans in the back, and the aroma was heavenly.

He joined me with my decaf chai latte, which I knew would be delicious—but I couldn't believe I had to forgo caffeine for months. His fully caffeinated beverage looked scrumptious.

"Things are getting serious with Joel?" I took a sip, and my eyes almost rolled back in my head from how good it was.

He shrugged then blew on his cappuccino. "I don't think so, but it's fun."

I toasted him. "To college and having fun." His laugh was infectious, and a few heads turned. I couldn't blame them. Max was hot. Not Phoenix-level hot, but no one compared to him.

I surveyed the room and, my heart skipped a beat when my gaze collided with a stormy silver one.

Phoenix was there, and he was headed my way.

CHAPTER ELEVEN

PHOENIX

Again with that guy? Aspen sat across from the dark-haired guy who liked to hang around her. Jealousy ripped through me like a defensive guard breaking through the line and slamming me with a bone-crushing tackle.

With laserlike intensity, I focused on Aspen. Our eyes met and held, and the rest of the busy chaos inside the restaurant ceased to exist. There was only her.

I held the to-go cup of coffee I'd just bought so tightly that it came dangerously close to exploding. I couldn't believe what I was seeing. Aspen and I'd had words last time she was hanging around that guy. I had no right to dictate who she was friends with, but Max was pushing the boundaries. He was into her, and I didn't blame him, but it didn't sit well with me, and my muscles tensed.

I crossed to their table then loomed over them, fighting the urge to knock the guy onto his back.

Aspen scowled, but I didn't budge. She brought out an odd possessive streak I'd never seen in myself before.

Max turned when he noticed her staring behind him with wide eyes.

I leaned down, resting my fists on their table, and got in his face. "What are you doing with my girlfriend?"

His eyes narrowed. "Having coffee. The concept should be a simple one. I would think even you could follow it."

I fisted his shirt before I even knew I was going to do it. Aspen leapt from her chair and rushed to get between us. She ducked under my arm and plastered herself against me, which was the only reason I let go of that tool friend of hers.

I wrapped Aspen in my arms, keeping her where she was, then bent to her ear to whisper, "Are you using this guy to try and make me jealous?"

"Why would I do that?" she muttered. "Nothing is going on between us, including friendship, which you made very clear. Max is my friend. Back off and stay out of my life."

I tilted her head back so she could see just how serious I was. "We have an agreement." I flicked my gaze down. She clearly got the meaning, evidenced by the flare in her eyes and the red infusing her cheeks. "And as far as anyone else is concerned, we're dating *exclusively*. I don't appreciate you cheating on me so publicly."

She raised an eyebrow. "Fake cheating? With my friend?"

"Fine." I grinned, and she chuckled. "Then I guess I should get to know your *friend* too."

"You're being an asshole."

She shoved at my chest, but I didn't budge. "I've never claimed to be anything else." I knew my reputation—it matched that of my brother and cousins. We didn't put up with anything. People bowed to us and did what we wanted, just because we were good athletes. It was messed up, but it'd been like that for as long as I could remember. The only difference was that our cousins had gotten cozy with their steady girlfriends. We treated them like the queens they were, but anyone else was fair game.

I released her, and she shoved me before huffing. I was angry and didn't want to take it out on her. But her friend was another story. I grinned down at him before pulling up a chair and joining them—looked like it was open season. "So Max, how do you know Aspen?"

He snorted and leaned back in his chair. "I don't see how that's any of your business."

Oh, this fucker has a death wish. "You want to rethink that answer?"

"We have art class together," Aspen snapped, "and you already know we live in the same dorm this semester."

I snapped my focus to her. *This semester?* I wanted to question her, but not in front of Max, who probably wanted to get in her pants. I would revisit the comment later. For the time being, I wanted to toy with him.

"So… art." I skimmed his ripped skinny jeans. I hated to say it because not having money was a real thing that affected a lot of people, and my family would have been poor if not for Grandad, but I wanted him to get away from her. "You're majoring in how to be a starving artist?"

"And you're doing what? Putting all your hopes into maybe getting seen by an NFL scout?"

Yeah, he had my number. But I had his too. "Do you always ask other guys' girlfriends out? Cause it seems like you're waiting in the wings to take advantage of her if something goes wrong in her current relationship."

Something dark infused Max's eyes, and I paid closer attention. He squinted at me for a moment. "Funny thing is that I do hang out with girls that are in relationships. And you know what happens?" He leaned forward. "They always confide in me and not the ones they're committed to. Wonder why that is?"

What the actual fuck? I growled, imagining pounding his face.

He turned to Aspen. "Hey, sweetie. I'm going to take off. Seems you two have a few things to catch up on."

"Ah, no. There's nothing Phoenix and I need to talk about. I'll go with you."

She stood, following Max's lead, but there was no way I would let him get the upper hand. I clapped my hand onto his shoulder and held him in place as Aspen moved slightly ahead, not realizing what I'd done. I crowded Max, towering over him in both height and bulk. "Better watch your back." Then I released him. He jogged to Aspen's side, falling into step with her as they headed toward her dorm.

I couldn't believe she was out with that guy. What was even worse was how much it bothered me. I grabbed my to-go cup and tore out of The Spot. I had to get home, anyway. But later, Aspen and I would have words.

Back at the house, I passed several teammates hanging out and playing video games on the first floor. The house was huge, and most first- and second-year students stayed there. Upper-level students could move off campus, and next year, I knew Cole and Riley were planning on getting a place. Damon and Skylar probably were too.

They'd asked if Shane and I wanted to move in, but I was on the fence. There wouldn't be a cost because Cole was purchasing the place. He and Damon didn't have their trust funds yet, but Uncle Lucas was a billionaire, and they had their own money from him.

Things were different for Shane and me. And now, with Aspen and the baby, I wasn't sure what would happen.

I dumped my backpack onto my bed and riffled through it for the book I was supposed to read but was too stupid to start. I hated my learning disorder and that I had to share a portion of my secret with a stranger. This time, Stan, my advisor, had assigned a girl to tutor me. She was supposed to be here soon.

The door opened, and Shane lumbered in, looking exhausted.

"Where've you been? Tracey's?"

He scowled as he passed me to grab a book. "Why do you think I was with her? You made sure that relationship crashed and burned."

"Cut the crap. I know you've been with her since she dumped you in a text."

"Thanks to you." He got in my face. "If you hadn't lied to her, we would still be together."

"Until something else happened to threaten your potential in her eyes." I bumped him back with my chest. "But if you're okay with a gold-digger who's only interested in fame and fortune and doesn't stick around when things are rough, then don't let me stand in your way."

Shane paused, and I didn't like how he looked at me. That calculating, penetrating stare told me he was looking past my bullshit to try to see what I was pissed about. *News flash, bro, I'm still mad that you went back to her in any capacity and for any reason. Will you ever learn?*

"What's up with you?"

The change in his demeanor gave me whiplash. "If you were ever around, you would fucking know."

"I'm working my ass off. Maybe you would understand if you picked up the slack with our family instead of having your head up your ass."

I had no idea what he was talking about, but a soft knock on the door had me backpedaling fast. "Go. I'm not in the mood to have it out with you right now. I've got shit to do."

The last thing I needed was for him to know I was getting a tutor because I couldn't cut it on my own. He knew I couldn't get through some of the classes without help, but I didn't think he understood the extent of it.

We'd always been there for each other, like when we were little and he stuttered. If anyone made fun of him, our cousins and I would torment them so much that we developed a reputation not to mess with us. Eventually, Shane got over his speech impediment, but feeling like he wasn't good enough had left scars. I felt that more than he knew. If people discovered how hard it was for me to read a simple chapter, I would become the dumb jock Max had accused me of being, but to thousands of people.

I hated school—the academics, the sleepless nights, and the worry that I couldn't keep up. So when Shane stormed out and past the short brunette standing in the doorway with her hand raised to knock again, I was relieved.

I waved her in, not really looking at her. The door closed behind her, and I grabbed my book and shoved it in her direction. She took it timidly, and some of the red haze faded from my sight, and I looked closely at her. "Noel?"

"Hey, Phoenix." She cleared her throat. "I'm supposed to tutor you in lit and I think sociology?" The breathiness that was there a minute ago was gone.

I studied her as she nibbled on her lip, her eyes soft and dreamy. In high school, Noel Simon had been captain of the debate team, class president, and who knew what else. She was a brain with dark hair that fell in big curls around her shoulders and huge brown eyes. She wore the same round, wire-rimmed glasses from last year. She'd had a huge crush on me.

I grinned, turning on the charm. "Wow, it's good to see you. I didn't know you went to Thane."

"Yeah. It's great here. I love it." Her cheeks turned a deeper shade of red. "I saw your game Saturday. You were amazing. Even better than when we were in high school."

"Thanks." I motioned for her to take a seat in one of the chairs. "I have an unusual request. I need you to read this book to me since there isn't an audio recording." How that was possible, I wasn't sure, but I'd looked everywhere and no audio version existed. "I don't absorb the material very well when I read. I'm more of an auditory learner."

"Oh, sure." She got situated and opened the book to where I told her I'd left off.

I made myself comfortable with my legs stretched out on the bed and my back resting against the wall. If we could figure out how to fit in her reading those chapters to me, then all of the schoolwork I was behind on because of football, weightlifting, watching film, and the fights might be okay. I stood a chance at passing midterms. Maybe it would work out.

Finally, something was going my way.

CHAPTER TWELVE

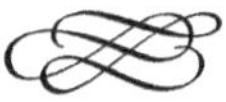

ASPEN

"He's such an asshole." I paced Max's dorm room. "I can't believe he talked to you that way. And the starving-artist comment..." I threw my hands up then planted them on my hips, glaring at him. "Does he not realize I'm an artist too?"

Max smirked. His eyes shifted from me to the mirror in the Jack-and-Jill bathroom he and his suitemates shared. With deft hands, he drew a thin line of black eyeliner under lashes too long to belong to a guy.

"That's not fair, either." I pointed to his eyes, heated about everything and unable to stop myself. What I was doing wasn't good. I had to stop complaining about the asshat. But—ugh—I couldn't stop thinking about him. The entire situation was a nightmare. And what made it worse was my sister had been on team Phoenix since she and Dane saw him play.

"What's not fair?" Max set the liner down and rested a lean hip against the counter.

I pointed to his gorgeous eyes. "That you have eyelashes that any girl would be jealous of."

"Honey"—Max shook his head—"you know that's not why

you're mad. And thank you." He batted his eyelashes then blew me a kiss.

I rolled my eyes at him but felt slightly lighter from him joking around. "I'm sorry." I wrung my hands, not knowing how to make what happened to him better.

Max sighed, squeezed my shoulders, and gently backed me out of the bathroom until we were at his bed. I climbed onto the mattress next to him, grabbing one of his fluffy throw pillows and hugging it to my stomach. I hated how out of control I felt.

"We're going to have a little heart to heart, baby girl. Now"—he patted my hand—"I'm well aware of the eye candy and can only imagine what it would be like to sleep with that guy. Wait"—a devious grin stretched his mouth—"let me imagine that for a hot minute."

"Stop it." I smacked him with the pillow and laughed. When his expression turned serious, I sank my teeth into my bottom lip. I wasn't sure I would like what he said next.

"You know I love you. In the short time I've known you, you've become one of my best friends. But honey, Phoenix isn't a guy you should be with. He's a walking billboard for bad attitude."

I loved that Max was looking out for me, but... "It's not that simple." I was surprised he hadn't heard about the baby already. But he didn't run with the same crowd as Phoenix's ex, despite casually dating one of the guy cheerleaders.

"It's never easy when the guy probably plays your va-jay-jay like a fine-tuned instrument. But you can't let someone treat you that way. He's possessive, jealous, controlling..." Max frowned. "Maybe those aren't actually bad things, but his attitude is, and you deserve better, sweetie."

He was correct on both counts. I dreamed of our only time together more often than I wanted to admit, and I did deserve better. All Phoenix and I seemed to do was argue. It terrified me that I would live my parents' life if I let him in too much, leading to me setting those boundaries earlier when I told him to leave me alone and that I wasn't his business anymore. But Max didn't understand our *other* connection, and it was time to let him in on that little not-so-secret news.

"I can't completely cut him out of my life because I'm pregnant, and he's the father."

Max's mouth dropped open, and his eyes whipped to my flat stomach before they returned to my face. He snapped his mouth shut with an audible pop. I swore I could see the wheels turning in his head before he let himself speak. "When did this happen?"

"Over the summer. July. I'm three months along." It was still weird to say it out loud. I wasn't used to it, but my reality solidified a little more each time.

"Don't kill me for asking this, but how will having a baby fit your future plans?"

"I haven't figured it out yet."

"Well, baby girl"—he made an O with his mouth—"I guess I shouldn't call you that anymore."

I snickered. "It doesn't bother me."

He took my hands in his warm ones and squeezed. "I'm always here to listen if you need a sounding board. And if you want to, you can tell Phoenix I'm gay."

"About that… why haven't you told him?"

He flashed a mischievous grin. "Him thinking I'm into you and competing with him is much more fun. He's all *grrr* and sexy. I like the visual." He shrugged. "Sue me."

"I like the visual, too, just not when he opens his mouth. If I could duct tape it closed, he would be just about everything I wanted." I giggled, knowing Max would understand my humor. "I just want to sleep with him, not let him say anything because he's always starting with me, and then have him leave.

Max pursed his lips. "Why don't you propose a deal between you two for sex? You're already pregnant. What would be the harm?"

"I…" I had no argument, especially since he wasn't the first person close to me who'd made that suggestion. Riley and Cass had spearheaded the argument to go for it. We fell into silence, and I let the idea roll around in my head. It's not as though I hadn't thought of it before, but to hear Max say it… *Why not?* "I'm not sure how that would work. Neither of us wants a relationship. The baby is literally the only thing we have in common."

"Just a little something to think about." He tugged my hand. "Come on. I'll walk you back to your room."

"Oh, right." I slid off the bed and went with him. "You have that date tonight. Don't do anything I wouldn't."

He hugged me and laughed. "That literally says do everything." He bopped my nose. "I approve. And trust me. I plan to do all that and much more. Joel is fine with a capital F."

Back in my room, I flopped onto my bed and pulled out my phone. My homework was done except for that last chapter I had to read, but I was too tired to do that and didn't want to. Instead, I called Regan.

"Hey." She sounded out of breath. "Everything okay?"

"Yep. Do you have a minute? I thought we could talk a little about the business."

"I've got five minutes, but then I'm packing to go to Paris with Dane and his family!"

"What?" I sat up, stunned. "When did this happen? And what about school?"

"It's only about ten days, and I'm frantically trying to find out my assignments so I can get as much of my school work done, so I'm not completely drowning in it when we get back. Or worse, doing homework while traveling."

I didn't know what to say. "That's amazing. I can't believe it. Why did they decide to go?" *And take you with*, but I didn't want to ask that.

"Dane's mom has some old college friends who live in

France, and one of them manages Louis Vuitton. She wants to go shopping and introduce me to the Paris fashion scene. It's going to be nonstop designers. I can't wait!"

"I'm so happy for you, Regan." I was also sad, but that was the self-pity talking. Her life was just beginning, and mine was stalled and uncertain. "We can talk when you're back. Take tons of pictures. Love you, sis."

"Thanks. I promise I'll call you as soon as we're back home."

We hung up, and I lay back down and stared at the ceiling. I wanted to ask her to come to my next doctor's appointment. It was all so scary, and I felt so alone. A small part of me thought about asking Phoenix, but based on his assholery earlier, I decided against it. I didn't want to give him any additional control over my life. Somehow, I felt like he would find new ways to torture me even more than nagging me to take the vitamins.

That left Mom. I toyed with the phone, unsure about calling. I'd tried to talk to them a few days ago. Dad was still so mad that he wasn't speaking to me. But they'd had more time to get used to me being pregnant, and I hadn't run home. Plus, they knew, whether it was true or not, that I had a boyfriend. Maybe they thought we would make things work.

Screw it. I pressed Mom's contact button then waited for her to answer. And waited… It rang for so long that I wasn't sure she was going to pick up. But she finally did and also sounded out of breath.

"Ew, Mom. Please tell me you ran for your phone."

She sighed. "I just got home from work and forgot my phone in the car when I brought the groceries in. That's it."

Thank God because the alternative had therapy written all over it.

"Is everything okay?"

I glanced out the large window to see a few groups of students walking. It was nice out. Maybe later, I would take a blanket out there and read my book outside instead of staying stuck in my claustrophobic dorm room.

"I'm good. Did you know Regan's going to Paris?" I couldn't help it, but I felt betrayed. It was stupid, and I was ashamed for even feeling that way. I wanted the best for my sis, even if it meant doing the business alone. For now, that was how I had to look at things because that ticking clock was only getting louder as each day passed and the baby's due date got closer.

"Yes, Debra called and asked if I would be okay with it. Of course, I said yes. Such a wonderful opportunity for your sister."

"It is." There was a beat of silence, and I didn't feel like filling it. *Why am I the last to know about this?*

"Aspen, what's bothering you?"

"Are you still mad at me?" I knew Dad was, but I wasn't going there. That would have started a whole different argument, and then she would hang up with me and find him to fight with before I even found the answer to my question.

"I'm working on it." She let go of a heavy sigh. "It's just not the situation I'd hoped for you. You're talented, and I know you have plans for your life. And the last thing I want is for you and that Phoenix boy to give up your dreams. Look what it did to your father and me."

"We're not going to give anything up." *Unless he does because of his grades.* I had no idea why he wouldn't talk to me or let me help him. The only time he'd been honest about what was bothering him was when he'd gotten drunk and come to my room that night. But whatever, that wasn't for me to fix. I would help him if he let me. And he wasn't going to, so that was that.

"I worry. Your father does too. It's not going to be easy. That's why I stayed home to take care of you girls."

I knew the story, and we didn't need to get into it. "I have a doctor's appointment coming up. Do you want to go with me?"

"I would love to, Aspen."

I sagged into my pillow, relieved that she hadn't asked why

Phoenix wasn't going to be there and that I didn't have to go alone.

We chatted for a few more minutes before I heard Dad yelling and Mom said she had to go.

Even with the doctor's appointment settled, I couldn't relax. The situation with Phoenix not being able to accept my help nagged at me far too much. *Screw it. I'm going to talk to him.*

It didn't take me long to get to his place, push my way inside the football house, and storm down the hall.

I jogged up the stairs toward Phoenix's room just as Shane was leaving. We didn't say anything to each other—in fact, he barely glanced at me, and I got the impression he didn't really see me. I hurried past him, grabbing the door to Phoenix's room before it shut. He'd barged into my business often enough, and turnabout was fair play.

But once I was inside, I thought my eyes were playing tricks on me. A cute brunette was in there, reading to him. I saw red. There were no words.

Phoenix sat up straight, coming off from where he'd been leaning back against the wall. "Aspen."

Him saying my name caused the brunette to stop reading. She just sat there, looking curious.

Screw it. I did have words after all. "What do you think you're doing in here with my boyfriend?"

"I—"

"Aspen," Phoenix growled.

I shook my head. "Nope. This is how things are going to go." I took the girl's arm and guided her toward the door. "Thanks for the help, but he won't be needing it anymore." Once she was through and I had the door shut, I crossed my arms over my chest and glared. I wasn't going to back down. "There is no room for negotiation, so don't even try to pull your alpha bull-shit with me. You will accept my help, or I won't tell you when or where or even about the doctor's appointments or the baby's progress." It was a low blow, but I had to get through his thick skull. We needed to find common ground.

A muscle jumped in his jaw, but he stood from the bed, picked up the book the girl had been reading, and handed it to me.

It was as much of an acceptance as I was going to get, but I would take the hard-won victory. I softened my voice as I said, "If I'm going to accept your help sometimes, then you need to do the same with me."

I got situated on the desk chair where the tutor had been, and he returned to his spot on the bed. "What is she helping you with? How many chapters a night, or do you want to change the original plan to something more frequent?" I caught and held his gaze. I was determined to do this.

He ran a hand over his face, exhaustion evident in the dark circles under his eyes. "It's been tough to find the time. If there was an audio version, I could listen while I run, but there isn't. Noel has been meeting with me once or twice a week in any window of time I find."

I could fix that. I had more time than he did. The problem was figuring out when we could sync up, and I refused to watch him let his grades suffer. "You have the rest of the book to finish?" At his nod, I flipped through the chapters. He was halfway through. "I'll read a few tonight and record the rest on my phone. I can send it to you. But"—I narrowed my eyes—"you will let me know when there is any new content you need read aloud, including emails or books like this. Got it?"

The lines around his mouth eased, and he nodded. "Sounds good. And Aspen"—he waited until he had my full attention—"thank you."

Warmth filled me because he'd finally put his trust in me for something that was such a touchy area. If only our battles would end so well every time.

CHAPTER THIRTEEN

PHOENIX

Grandad had called a midweek family dinner. He did that on occasion, and we all had to show up like we were marionettes on the strings he held. At least he'd given a few days' notice—he didn't always—and let us know the morning after Aspen had fired my tutor. I'd downloaded a few recordings from her for the reading assignment. Already, I could tell the arrangement would be a game changer.

I hit the button on my phone to connect to Shane while toeing on my shoes, waiting for him to answer. He did, at the last possible second before it went to voicemail.

"Hey." *Is that Mom's voice in the background?* "Want to ride together to go to family dinner tonight?"

"Can't. I'm already there."

"What the hell? You're never around, and then you take off for home without me? Did you even consider checking in to see about driving together?"

I didn't get it. Shane had been acting like such an asshole. We'd never gone that long without talking, and a part of me felt empty. "Is this still about Tracey?"

"Look." A door shut, and the background noise was even

more muffled. He must have gone to another room. "The shit with Tracey was wrong, and you know it. But that's not what this is about. I've been busy. We're not in high school anymore."

"Fuck you. Who the hell do you think you're talking to?" Definitely not his twin brother that had been through everything with him.

"It isn't anything personal."

There was a lack of heat behind his words that made me pause. Shane sounded tired. We ended the call, and I grabbed my wallet then headed to my SUV. I crossed paths with Cole, surprised to see him alone. We saw each other at football and in the gym every day, but it was different than back home, and a part of me missed that.

"You headed home too?" Cole tossed a bag into his backseat.

"Yeah, I've got dinner with Mom and Grandad tonight. Why are you?"

"Raelyn said she had some stuff for Riley. I had some extra time, so I said I would pick it up. Want to ride with me? Shane called to see if I'd left yet."

I pressed the lock button on my key fob. "Why did my brother ask you that?"

"He wanted to see if we could ride out together, and then the two of you would come back. Said he was exhausted and wanted you to drive him after dinner."

"Did he seem weird to you?"

Cole shrugged and got into his identical SUV as I slid into the passenger seat. "A little withdrawn, but I think the shit with Tracey is still bothering him." We pulled onto the road, heading toward the highway that would take us to Hidden Valley.

"He's better off without her." I'd done what I had to do. We were family, all of us, and we looked out for each other. If I hadn't done it, I had a feeling Cole or Damon would have found a way to get them to break up. The girl was toxic, and we all knew it.

"I'm not arguing with that. But you know Shane. He pulls back when something heavy is on his mind. He'll come around."

"I know. It just seems like something else is going on." Then again, I'd been in my head a lot, too, with everything happening with Aspen and that Max guy, who seemed to be around her way too often.

"What's going on with you and Aspen?"

"I don't know. Between studying, practices, lifting, and fights, I haven't had much time to talk with her."

"What about the doctor appointments? You go to those, right?"

Oh shit. "I haven't even thought about it. I've been trying to make sure I have enough money for whatever she needs for the baby or in general. Her parents are a mess, and I'm not sure they'll help… And it's my responsibility."

We drove by the exit that would have taken us to the cove, and what had happened there with Aspen over the summer assaulted my senses. I wanted, more than I was ready to admit to myself, to hold her in my arms again.

"That's pretty fucking understanding of her."

"What are you talking about?" I glared at Cole as he swept his dark hair from his forehead.

"She's going to those appointments alone?"

"Maybe." *Probably.*

"I'm just saying, it's a lot. She's probably scared. You should go with for moral support."

I let my head thud back against the headrest. He was right. I hadn't been thinking about that, only the money problems we were both facing. "I'll talk to her."

I added that to my long to-do list. Of course, it was going to the top. I only hoped it would be enough. Why Aspen and I couldn't find common ground about anything other than when we touched was challenging.

"Damon mentioned you were buying a house next year that Riley and Skylar were also moving into."

His green eyes pierced me before returning to the road. "You and Shane too."

"Yeah, Damon said that too."

Cole frowned, but I didn't elaborate. Aspen was due next semester. I wasn't sure of the exact date. I would have to find out, which only made me feel worse. No wonder she was so prickly around me and let that opportunist hang around her all the time. I hadn't been there for her, not really. I need to change that.

We turned off the exit and made small talk for the ten minutes it took to get to Grandad's, where I thanked him for the lift and headed inside.

Grandad lived in a neighborhood similar to ours but that wasn't on the beach. His house was a giant brick monstrosity that hadn't been updated since Nona was alive. I let myself in then called a hello.

"Phoenix." Mom rounded the corner with a big smile and deep circles hanging under her eyes.

"Hi, Mom." I pulled her in for a tight squeeze. It drove both Shane and me crazy that she worked so hard.

"Phoenix, my boy." Grandad shook my hand then yanked me in for a bear hug.

I caught Shane's eyes over his shoulder. He looked just as tired as Mom. And he wore the pouty expression that meant he had to do something he hated. I brushed it off because it was probably caused by being forced to family dinner. I felt the same way. I loved my family, but Grandad was overbearing. With everything we had going on at school, midweek dinners were inconvenient.

It also meant he probably had something up his sleeve, and I didn't like it. Apparently, my brother didn't either. With one glance, the animosity between us melted away, and it was just

Shane and me like it should have been the whole time. After that small exchange, Shane went into the den, where the faint sound of a game played on the TV.

Grandad put his hand on the side of my check then smacked it harder than necessary. It was a sly move he liked to do that looked friendly, but the sting said otherwise. I grit my teeth as Mom slipped from the room and out the front door, no doubt for a cigarette. She had been born a rebel. I wasn't the only one who noted her absence—Grandad took full advantage.

"What's this I hear about your failing grades?" His bushy white eyebrows hung low over blue eyes that had lost some of their color due to age, amplifying the map of wrinkles on his face.

There was my answer for why we were having family dinner in the middle of the week. Grandad liked to use in-person tactics to keep us on track. "It's just an adjustment to forty hours dedicated to athletics and finding time for classes and homework."

"That's life, kid. You sink or swim. And we're not quitters. Are we?" He tapped my cheek again for good measure.

"I've got it under control. I can turn it around."

"I'll be keeping an eye on things. I better not see any more failing grades." He waited a beat, and I nodded. "Now, go get your mother. We're about to eat."

I went onto the cement porch to find mom resting her elbows on the railing, a cigarette dangling from her fingers. "You need to quit that."

She grinned. "I'm down to one a day. Working on it. But"—she gestured toward the house—"you know."

I did. Grandad was being his usual self, pissing off everyone in the house with his domineering attitude.

"How's school?" She took a drag and turned her head to blow it away from me.

"School is what it is." I had to tell her about Aspen and the baby, and I guessed there was no time like the present. "I need to talk to you about something." We hadn't talked much since school started.

She snubbed out the cigarette then waved away my words. "Don't worry. I know you'll get your grades up."

I frowned, and she rolled her eyes.

"My dad keeps me informed of your progress. I know you'll get it under control." She rolled her neck, cracking it, which she did when she was stressed.

"What's going on? You look exhausted, and with Shane and me out of the house, I would've thought you could cut your bills." With us at school, she didn't have to pay as much for electricity or groceries. That one was the worst, but she refused to let us help out. We tried to sneak food into the fridge sometimes, but she would get upset, saying that our job was school and sports, hers was to work and pay the bills, and she didn't appreciate us trying to do her job for her. I loved that about Mom. Even though she was a rebel, she had a good head on her shoulders and had always made sure we were taken care of above everything else.

And soon, it would be my turn to do that—for her, Aspen, and the baby. "We should probably go in before Grandad has to come out here and get us for dinner." Mom shuddered.

Yeah, I didn't want to deal with that either. I still needed to tell her about the baby and Aspen, but that window had closed. I would tell her soon before Shane opened his big mouth. Normally, my brother was good for keeping secrets, but because of the lie I'd told Tracey, I wasn't sure if he would get back at me. Telling our family about the baby before I could would definitely accomplish that.

I suffered through dinner then got in the car with Shane to head back to school while Mom went in the other direction, toward home. Once we were on the highway, I tried to talk to him. "Where've you been lately?" I missed my brother, and not just because he could help me with classes.

"Just taking care of some personal stuff."

He isn't going to talk to me? Fine. I'll keep all the mess in my life to myself too. Not that he asked.

Throughout dinner, Shane had been quiet too. It was probably about a chick, and he didn't want Grandad to know. Couldn't blame him. There were lots of things I didn't want Grandad to know.

CHAPTER FOURTEEN

ASPEN

I threw an envelope filled with money onto my desk. "If Phoenix sends me one more of these, I'll shove them up his ass." There was even more cash than the last time.

"I think you should keep it." Max set his sketchbook on the bed, mischief dancing in lined eyes. "You deserve it for carrying the devil's spawn. The kid's horns are probably gonna tear up your uterus."

I grunted then fell onto the small mattress next to him. He put his arm around me, and I leaned against him. He'd been calling Phoenix the devil since our run-in at the coffee shop, making jokes about him left and right.

"I don't want anything from him. I'm giving the money back."

"Listen to me, baby girl." Max hugged me tight, resting the side of his head against the top of mine. "You know you're going to need stuff for the kid. My older sister has kids, and she has one of those baby front packs, some bouncy thing, a jumping saucer thing with toys all around it, a swing, crib, diapers, and formula. None of it was cheap. Take the money. He owes you."

I covered my face with my hands. "I haven't thought that far ahead. I'll need a place to stay and probably a babysitter, too, so I can try and go to class. I don't know. I might have to drop out."

"Don't think that far ahead." Max shook his head. "Let's just go with what we know. You're going to need some stuff. He's giving you money. We're using that, and if you need more to pay for a place to live, then we'll hit him up for more. You're not alone in this. Let him help you, at least financially."

"I hate relying on others. Besides my sister, I never have before. But… my school bill is higher from losing the diving scholarship." I supposed I could hold onto the money and use it only if absolutely necessary. I didn't make that much at the diner. Not enough.

"Then it's decided. You're keeping the devil's money."

It bothered me. I didn't like taking handouts. Even though what Max said made sense. I could accept only some of the money for the baby, but that was it. Maybe a tiny bit if I couldn't make my school bills, but I would pick up extra shifts and do everything I could before I gave in and did that. I had to admit that it was nice to know a safety net was there.

I shook my head. "I'm giving some of it back. I'm keeping only enough to provide for the baby's necessities and ensure that I don't end up homeless." He'd given me way more money than I would need.

"If it makes you feel better, put what you don't think you'll need into a savings account for the kid."

"That's not a bad idea. But I'm going to tell Phoenix to stop giving me these envelopes." I didn't like it. "If I can get the big jerk to pay attention to me."

Max snorted a laugh. "The guy can't take his eyes off you."

"I've run into him on campus twice. Once, he pretended he was reading something on his phone and passed without looking up. And the other time, when I was leaving class, he was waiting outside another room, probably for whatever chick is shining his Heisman these days." I was embarrassingly aware of how jealous I sounded. And I was. There was a crazy attraction between us, and I even liked how he wanted to take care of me. But I had to question how much of that was because he was into me versus him wanting to make sure our baby was okay. It bothered me. And when he opened his mouth, we had problems.

"If he is paying attention to another girl, we'll find ways to make his life very difficult. But I genuinely don't think he sees anyone but you."

I wasn't so sure. But it helped that Max understood—of course he did. He was that cliché, the perfect guy hidden inside a gay best friend. I was lucky to have become friends with him.

"I was dating a total smoke show before Joel. Did I ever tell you about Bruce?"

"No, you haven't, but please do." I needed a distraction.

Max sighed, and his head thumped against the wall. "He was beautiful. All this golden skin and just... beautiful to look at. When he paid me a little bit of attention, I was in, and I mean like a little puppy following him around for whatever scraps he would throw my way."

I made myself sit up, and his arm fell away. Pivoting on the bed, I sat cross-legged to see his expression. "That doesn't sound like you."

He pursed his lips. "Not now. But back then, I was head over heels for Bruce." With a shake of his head, he gave me a small smile. "Our relationship was toxic. He treated me like I was disposable unless he wanted something from me."

"What do you mean?"

"We would go out on a date, which was basically back to his place. In public, he barely acknowledged me. But he would be at my door late at night, looking for a hookup. I thought we were dating. He was busy because he was a music major, and I had another friend who barely had time to breathe."

I leaned forward, wondering where he was going with this. "Okay, so that wasn't the deal with Bruce?"

"No." A self-deprecating laugh slipped past his lips. "Turned out he wasn't a music major, and the reason why he was so busy was that he was in a relationship—with a woman. That was the reason he ignored me in public. I was just his dirty little secret and late-night booty call."

"What an ass. I hope you told him off in front of his girlfriend." My nails dug into the comforter. I was more than a little angry. "Does he still go here?" I wanted to pay him a little visit too.

"I confronted him, and he dumped me. I went a little crazy and considered stalking the guy and his girlfriend, but I didn't. I got drunk instead."

"If only..."

He winked. "As soon as the demon's spawn is born, there's a bottle of Patron with your name on it."

"It's a deal." It was still so early, but I couldn't wait to have my body back. Not that I didn't already love the little peanut growing inside me, because I did, but being exhausted, puking, and the way my body was going to change sucked. I could have done without those things and being unable to dive. At least there was surfing. I would continue to surf unless the doc said to stop.

Max tossed his pencil near his discarded sketchpad. "Let's go to the fights tonight."

I'd been to the underground fights before—I'd learned about them from one of the football players after I went to find Phoenix to talk to him about being pregnant. It'd left an impression, and a tremor swept through me at the memory of how he looked in the ring—like a man made in the image of the gods as he threw one powerful punch after another, kicking ass and looking good as he did it. "I'm not sure if that's a good idea."

He ruffled my hair, scooted off the bed, and went straight to my closet. "We can go incognito, bet a bunch of his money on the other guy, then celebrate with a shopping spree when he gets his ass kicked."

I didn't want to admit that watching Phoenix fight was a turn-on, but Max was probably already aware of that. He was hot on the football field—they were undefeated so far—and in the ring. The guy was mesmerizing, and I knew Max wasn't immune. "Okay, I'll go."

"Good, but you need to get dolled up. I'm not taking you to the fights in your ratty-ass sweatpants."

CHAPTER FIFTEEN

PHOENIX

I could not for the life of me figure out what the fuck Aspen was doing there. The warehouse was full and going strong because of the packed schedule for fight night. I moved around Damon for a better view, and sure as shit, she was talking with that opportunist, Max. That fucker would regret moving in on her.

Max wasn't the only one paying her attention. Several guys around them were looking. It was hard not to. She was naturally beautiful with skin that glowed and looked soft as hell—it was—and the light catching her blond hair drew further notice. I bet that was why Max had pulled her close to him. I would have done the same thing. The difference was that Aspen was mine, which I still had trouble acknowledging, but the fierceness of how much I wanted her—and the baby growing in her belly—shocked me.

Damon continued talking over the crowd's roar, but I heard nothing. *Goddammit.*

"Hey." Damon grabbed my shoulder, pulling my attention back to him. "How the fuck did you end up fighting Flynn?"

I was in a shit mood. I was fighting Jake Fucking Flynn, a

guy who had gone fifteen and zero in the last three months. The dude could bench-press Shane and me together. On top of that, everything was going to shit with Aspen. She was probably betting on my opponent. Hell, if I were smart, I would too.

"I asked to go against him. I need a good fight to get all the shit going on in my life out of my system." I meant not doing well in school and Aspen taking up entirely too much of my mind. The fact that she came to the fight with that little fuck, Max, made me think he was there with her just to rub my nose in it.

Damon followed my line of sight and spotted Aspen. "So… a girl."

I glared at him. "Not just a girl."

He slapped my chest with the back of his hand. "I get it, man. But you need to get your head in the fight because if you don't, Flynn's gonna lay you out."

I didn't care. I should have, but all I saw was how Max's arm curled around Aspen. How I'd managed to spot her in the first place was one of those crazy things I couldn't explain

Damon laughed. "I don't think Max is a threat."

I didn't give a fuck what Damon thought about it or how he knew him. I glanced at the clock. It wasn't time for my fight yet, and there was no way I could let it go. I shook his hand from my bicep and shoved through the crowd. Someone shouted my name. People tried to get my attention. I ignored everyone but her.

The crowd moved for me as I made my way to her, and it wasn't long before I was at her side. I grabbed her shoulder and turned her toward me, stopping her mid-conversation. And when she turned, I wrapped my arm around her waist, shaking Max's hold loose. She had to have gone with me out of shock more than anything.

Strawberries and vanilla invaded my senses, and the crowd faded. All I could see was her. *Why does she have this effect on me?*

My hands were on her hips, holding her in place, close but not too close.

"You shouldn't be here." I bared my teeth at her, consumed by too many emotions. "And now, I see what you're doing with all the money I've been giving you," I growled the last bit against the edge of her ear, so no one else heard. "Pissing it away and probably betting against me."

She laughed, and I leaned back. Her smile didn't reach her eyes. They were snapping with an angry flare of fire. "I never asked you for any of that. Nor were there stipulations. I was wrong, though—there are. Invisible ones. What else aren't you telling me about those little envelopes and what they mean?"

I didn't like where the conversation was going. It hit too close to home, bringing up a ton of unwanted memories of Mom arguing with Shane and my sperm-donor father.

"Guess we'll have to talk about that later." But the thought of it made me angry. I shouldn't have cared if she spent the money however she wanted, as long as enough went toward the baby and her cost of living expenses. But she was right. I hadn't said anything when I'd shoved those white envelopes under her door.

"Whatever." She frowned.

I wanted to run my thumb over her soft lower lip. Fuck, she was a distraction I didn't need. My fight was about to start. "Go home, Aspen. This isn't a safe place for you."

She tilted her head back so our eyes met and held, and sun-bleached strands tumbled down her back. "Funny. Because last we talked, you had no say in my life." She jabbed my chest with a finger. "And that's how you wanted it too. I'm to stay out of your life. Which means you damn well better stay out of mine."

But I don't want that. The dark-haired dweeb moved closer to Aspen, but I ignored him. There was a reason I wasn't mentioning him. I didn't want to kill the guy, although I kind of did.

"Why do I have to keep reminding you that we're dating?" The whole thing was weird as shit. "There are many girls who would jump at the chance, but you…"

"You want to date me?" She quoted the word date. I got it. We were in public, which was why I didn't add the fake part either. "Then you get all of me, including studying." She raised her eyebrows.

No fucking way. "That's taking things too far. But there are plenty of other areas that aren't. Leave, Aspen," I growled, closing the distance between us.

"Go fuck yourself, Phoenix," she hissed.

I didn't want that smart little mouth of hers to come up with any other complaints or rules. I kissed her to shut her up—and to send a message to everyone around her.

My mouth slanted over hers, punishing, controlling, and coaxing her to respond. I hadn't needed to. She melted against me, winding her arms around my neck and tangling her fingers in my hair.

Her lips parted on a sigh. Sparks danced between us, and my insatiable need for her exploded into a wave of desire. I lost myself in the sweetness of her mouth and the soft curve of her hips as I pressed her against me. Our surroundings faded. There was only her.

A sharp tug on my shoulder brought a slice of reality back, and I reluctantly broke the kiss. The increased noise from the crowd as the announcer shouted into a mic rushed back in with alarming force. Then Damon pulled me back, and my hands fell away from her, a sense of emptiness following when space expanded between us. I didn't want to leave her, especially not there, where so many people could bump into her or take advantage of her. She needed to be tucked into my side, where no one could reach her.

Damon tugged on my shoulder again, breaking my connection to Aspen. I let her go, and my attention snapped to him.

"You've got to get in the ring."

My hands were taped. All I had to do was take off my shirt, and I was ready. I took one more glance at Aspen as she moved back to Max's side, and all the anger at our situation trickled back in. Good. Flynn's face was going to take the edge off.

"Goddammit." I didn't want to back down from arguing with Aspen that she shouldn't be there, but when I glanced at the stage, Flynn was already in the ring.

CHAPTER SIXTEEN

ASPEN

Phoenix was unstoppable in the ring. And that kiss. I kept touching my swollen lips. Even Max had whistled, a spark of heat in his eyes. I knew it wasn't directed at me, and I laughed. We hadn't had time to talk or dissect Phoenix's Neanderthal behavior. I was glad for that because he left me as confused as always.

I couldn't take my eyes off him. Fear and desire held me rooted in place. The crowd was nuts. People were screaming and chanting both of the fighters' names. And his opponent—I didn't know what Phoenix was thinking. The guy was a giant. I was legit terrified.

Phoenix was a beast, but his opponent was a couple of inches taller and had at least fifty pounds of muscle on him. He looked like he'd walked straight out of one of those heavyweight boxer movies.

But Phoenix had speed over his opponent and evaded as many hits as he could, ducking and weaving. He was all muscle, power, sinew, and sweat. And I couldn't take my eyes off him.

Phoenix threw a right and left hook then danced out of reach. His opponent—Jake Flynn, from what the announcer said

—shook off the punches. I watched Phoenix closely, having learned more about him just from the football game and this fight. He analyzed his opponents and then exploited them for all they were worth. He saw things I was sure few others did and employed bursts of speed that left my head reeling.

"Max!" A shrill voice tore my gaze away from the ring for a split second when a tall, thin guy wrapped Max in a hug.

When he pulled back, Max made quick introductions.

"Hi, Elias," I said, a shiver of dislike running down my spine. We'd seen each other on campus and in a class before, and yes, I was going out on a limb, but I knew we wouldn't be friends. Something sparked in Elias's eyes, too, but he gave me a partial smile then leaned into Max's other side.

A flurry of movement caused my focus to jump back to the ring, and with Max's friend forgotten, I waited with bated breath as the fight ensued.

Jake struck out. The punch was sloppy, and Phoenix easily blocked it then delivered one back that stunned his opponent, if only for a fraction of a second, with the strength behind it. Jake's confidence appeared shaky as Phoenix moved in and out. His endurance was higher, his skills sharper. Every once in a while, Jake would get a punishing blow in. Phoenix shook them off as if they were nothing. They weren't, though, and my heart was in my throat.

Finish this. I wanted him out. Safe. I shouldn't have cared, but for some stupid reason, I did.

He moved in, hitting Jake with a right cross then a left hook. Immediately, he danced out of reach. Again, he repeated the same move, looking for Jake's tells.

Jake retaliated. Phoenix blocked the jab then retaliated aggressively. He seemed to want to shake Jake's confidence further.

Max's hand gripped mine, and I squeezed so hard he had to pry my fingers off. I gave him a shaky grin before jerking my gaze back to the ring. There was blood on both guys' faces. My stomach was a mess. *Finish this, Phoenix.*

A girl not far from where I stood was screaming and jumping up and down. There was more chanting. The crowd seemed to press forward, the aggression of the fight affecting the audience.

Minutes passed, and Phoenix delivered a brutal combination that caused Jake to stagger back and drop to a knee. He didn't get up. The ref counted him off. And when he reached ten, the fight was over.

The announcer held Phoenix's arm up and called the fight. Our eyes met and held, making me dizzy with desire. Watching him had been incredible, and he was so freaking hot. But I recognized the adrenaline pumping through his body for what it was. If he caught up with me, I wouldn't be able—or want—to stop the inevitable from happening. There was too much heat and lust between us.

I shivered, wanting to tempt fate and wait for him to come to me. But it wasn't smart. We had too many problems that sex would only complicate. And as my adrenaline faded, exhaustion crept in.

I needed to get out of that stifling and overcrowded place. I tugged on Max's sleeve, and he turned from talking with his guy friend. "Hey, I'm going to head out."

"Oh, yeah." He glanced back Elias, and I thought I saw something between them. "I'll go with you."

"No." I made a point of looking at his friend. "You stay. There's no reason for you to go with me. I'll grab an Uber. And I'm wiped out. I need to crash."

Max frowned but must have seen how tired I was. He pulled me in for a hug. "Text me when you're back at the dorms and in your room, so I know you made it safely."

I squeezed him back. "I will." I waved bye to his friend then hurried toward the area where bets were taken. I needed to get out fast before Phoenix found me. I hit the Uber app and called for a ride.

It took some shoving and squeezing to move through the crowd. I finally reached the enormous guys that acted like security around the bookie.

Behind the table, a huge guy regarded me. A large snake tattoo climbed the side of his neck and disappeared under his shirt. Intense black eyes met mine, and I shivered. He looked like someone I wouldn't want to run into in a dark alley.

I gave him my ticket, and he grinned, cold and calculating. When he spoke, his deep voice cut through the noise and held me captive.

"Jake was favored to win. Since you bet on Phoenix, you tripled your money."

My jaw dropped. I snapped it shut then nodded. He counted out the cash and handed it to me. Before leaving, I tucked it into the front pocket of my jeans. I needed to get out of there, not only because of the large amount of cash on me but because I could sense Phoenix getting closer. I'd worn a lightweight zip hoodie and flipped the hood up to cover my hair, hoping it would work as a disguise so he couldn't spot me, then headed for the exit.

I was almost out of there when I squeezed through a group of guys, and a brunette whirled around. We made eye contact, and a heavy weariness settled over me. Suddenly, I wished that Phoenix had found me. Then he could go at Jillian, and I could make my escape.

Jillian yanked a tall blonde close. "Look at the groupie that showed up tonight."

They zeroed in on me, but I wasn't backing down. "Why are you talking about yourself?" I widened my eyes, feigning innocence. "Is it because you're trying to make a statement?"

"Hardly. I'm not the one trapping Phoenix." They shared a look then laughed before Jillian got in my face. "Phoenix may want you as a little plaything for now, but there's no way he'll stick around, especially when you get fat."

I rolled my eyes. "Keep telling yourself that." I snapped my fingers in her face as I sidestepped her. "Better yet, why don't you tell him what you think? He should be heading this way."

It worked like a charm. Jillian's gaze jerked over my shoulder, and I squeezed through the rest of the crowd. I had no idea how close Phoenix was, but I could bet he was nearby by the way the hairs on the back of my neck stood at attention.

My phone vibrated, and I checked, finding a notice that my ride was there. I hurried to get into my driver's red Corolla, gave him the dorm address, and rested against the leather seat.

When I returned to my room, I changed, shut off the light, and crawled into bed.

There was noise in the hallways, given that it was the weekend. I grabbed my phone. pulled up the white noise app, and selected ocean sounds. My eyes drifted shut as the soothing rhythmic back and forth of rolling waves filled the dark space. I snuggled deeper under the covers, trying to push all thoughts of Phoenix away, but I couldn't stop thinking about our time at the cove. Coupled with how he'd kissed me tonight and watching him fight, there was no way I could exorcise him from my mind.

CHAPTER SEVENTEEN

PHOENIX

I lost track of Aspen when I stepped out of the ring. Damon clapped me on the back, and a rush of adrenaline surged through me. I was still pumped from the fight. It wasn't a good idea to go find her. Not yet. I needed to calm down some.

"Man, I shouldn't have doubted you, but the size of that guy." Damon whistled. "Fucking fantastic match."

"Thanks." It bothered me that Cole and Shane weren't there. Cole had stepped away from the fights—they were a risk to both college and career, and I probably should have followed his lead, but that wasn't an option for me to stop right now. I had enough for school, but I worried about supporting more than just myself.

There were a few more fights, so I hung back with Damon. "Did you place a bet?"

Damon's grin was wicked. "You know I did. All on you. Guess who was favored to win?"

"Not me." I grinned. He had to have tripled his money. "Where's Sky?" The two of them were usually glued at the hip in their free time.

"Out with Riley and Cass tonight."

He and Sky were super tight, just like Cole and Riley were. "Does it bother you to be here? You weren't scheduled to fight."

"Nah. They wanted to do a girls' night, and since Shane hasn't been around… and Cole had to fly out of town with our dad."

He didn't need to say anything more. I knew that Cole getting along better with their dad still bugged him. Everything that had happened with Riley her senior year had only brought Cole and their dad closer, and I understood how Damon felt. Between Shane and me, I knew my brother would cave and let our dad in if an opportunity ever arose. Not me. The man was dead to me.

Damon and I stuck around for a while. Then he got a text from Sky saying she was headed back. We split up, he left, and I went to look for Aspen, unable to deny the possibility of seeing her any longer.

I pushed through the crowd. When people realized it was me, they tried to stop me to congratulate me on the fight. I said thanks and moved on quickly, feeling the window to catch her slipping away. I spotted Max but no Aspen.

And instead of finding her with him, I came face-to-face with her new boyfriend making out with some guy. I had no idea what was going on. I smacked Max on the shoulder. He turned around, and I immediately got in his face.

"What the fuck do you think you're doing?"

I didn't care if the guy swung for both fences, but if he was banging Aspen, he'd better be upfront with her.

"Aspen took off, and we"—he pointed between us—"have nothing to talk about." Max matched my move and got within an inch of my face. "So fuck off."

"Yeah, I don't think so." My hands flexed at my sides. It took everything in me not to lay the guy out. But something stopped me… maybe the confusion about why he was with another guy. "Does Aspen know your mackin' on some guy?"

A dark laugh spilled from Max's mouth. "Aspen's not my type, but if it keeps her away from you, a guy who has done nothing but hurt her, then I'll set her up with every single straight guy I know."

Aspen's attitude toward me about Max, then Damon's comment about how I didn't have to worry, filtered through my mind, staying my reaction. Max took the opportunity and stormed away. I was left with the guy Max had been making out with. He eyed me with interest. I turned and headed for the exit, wanting to pull my hair out. She made me so crazy I wasn't seeing things clearly. And that didn't happen to me.

It made me think about how much I really needed to stay away from her. Even though I wanted to go talk to her, I shouldn't. I had enough going on with school and football, and after dinner, Grandad had hit me up to make some deliveries for his company. As if I had the time for that. He wouldn't accept any answer but yes—he was a hard-ass like that—stating that the business would fall to Shane and me, and we needed to know every aspect of it, inside and out.

Screw that. I didn't want his business. Everything in my life was leading up to the NFL. And if I got injured or something else happened, then I would find another job that involved football. Sportscasting, analytics, coaching, whatever, just so long as I was still part of the game I was destined for. His property management company could bite me.

The drive back to the house was uneventful. I passed a few of the other guys and distractedly responded to their greetings or questions. I wanted more than anything to go to Aspen, to talk to her and find out what game she was playing with Max. Or maybe she didn't know he was into guys.

The truth was probably that I was the idiot, the only one that hadn't connected the dots. But she made me crazy. I couldn't think straight around her, and it shook me up. If she could affect me that way, it could eventually bleed onto the field, and I couldn't risk losing my ability to read the field, the plays, and the game's subtleties. Fuck that.

I had to stick to my original plan and help with our kid, provide for him or her, and not get involved with Aspen. If only I could get her out of my head.

In my room—Shane was absent again—I stripped off my clothes and headed to the shower. I did everything I could to block Aspen from my thoughts as pink-tinged water swirled around the drain until it disappeared. Water beat down on me, soothing sore muscles. I had to keep it together.

With a towel wrapped around my waist, I went back to my room and got dressed. As I pulled my shirt over my head, there was a hard knock at my door. My mind leapt with the hope that it was her, and I frowned. I had to get control of myself. Maybe going to the gym would help.

When I opened the door, I saw the last person I expected to be standing there. Grandad walked in with an air of authority, and I closed the door behind him. *What could he possibly want this late at night?*

"I have a proposition for you."

CHAPTER EIGHTEEN

ASPEN

That kiss was epic. I touched the pads of my fingers to my lips, remembering every second of his possessive touch. If we got along intellectually and emotionally as well as we did physically, things would be much easier.

I tugged the covers tightly around me, needing sleep over the after-party at the cove my roommate and her friends were attending, possibly with Phoenix in attendance. Would he think about me? The only thing that kept me sane was our fake-dating pact. With that in place, he couldn't mess around with any other girl. The thought of him with anyone else felt like a dagger through my heart, and it shouldn't have. We weren't even friends.

Eventually, I fell into a deep sleep, but Phoenix's reach was absolute even there. Dream Phoenix was just as sexy but not as combative.

I dreamed of a house on the beach with a lap pool and another one with a sun shelf and waterfall. In my arms, I held a little girl who had blond curls and big blue eyes streaked with silver. She looked like both of us and cooed happily as I set her in a crib for a nap. The room was white with pops of light pink, beautifully decorated and just the right size.

"Aspen."

Phoenix called for me, and I quietly shut the door then tiptoed downstairs, where I turned on the baby monitor.

"Our little princess is napping?"

I laughed, and he pulled me into his arms. "Soon. And what're you doing home?"

"We had meetings today. I was able to get in an hour in the gym then thought I would surprise you."

He looked just as fierce as he had our freshman year but somehow older and even more muscular. In our perfect dream world, I knew he'd been drafted early and was a starting quarterback on a team he loved. Our house was stunning, and I had help, so I didn't have to take care of it all myself.

"I thought we could have lunch outside."

He grabbed the monitor and pulled me close, leading me through the accordion glass doors that took us to the larger pool. The table was set for two, and soft music played through the speakers. "What's this about?"

"It's me wanting to spend time with you." He cupped my face and leaned in for a brief kiss. I always wanted more. "I love you, Aspen. Marrying you was the best decision I've ever made."

"Even better than the early draft?" I teased. I knew what his answer was, but it was nice to hear.

"Even better. You and our little girl are my entire world."

In the safety of his embrace, I forgot about the lunch he'd had set up and pulled him down for a kiss, losing myself in the magic between us.

A crash sounded, and I jerked away. Laughter grew louder as someone passed by my door, and a deep sadness filled me at being ripped from the fantasy I'd created. Gentle Dream Phoenix clashed with the violence of the ring and his reoccurring presence there.

I wasn't stupid and knew that the money he was giving me had to come from fighting. He was making sure I had enough by accepting and giving beatings, by putting his future on the line, risking injury every time. I turned on my side as a wave of unease washed over me. I didn't want to be a factor in him losing everything.

Maybe I'm being too harsh on Phoenix. I couldn't ignore how much I missed him.

CHAPTER NINETEEN

PHOENIX

proposition? I stood facing my grandad in the middle of my room not long after the fight with Jake Flynn had ended. Shane, of course, was nowhere to be found, and I had a bad feeling about what I was about to hear.

I gestured to one of the chairs, and he lowered himself into it. I took the one opposite him, suspecting I might want to sit while hearing him out. It was late, and my anxiety had spiked when he appeared out of the blue. "What's this proposition?"

The mini fridge was to my right, and I leaned over and grabbed a water, lifting it to see if he also wanted one. He shook his head, and I closed the door. I twisted off the cap and downed half the contents as I waited for him to enlighten me about why the fuck he was in my room at midnight.

"You know how important my company is to me."

I nodded, leaning back in my chair and settling in for a long speech. Grandad loved to soapbox. He meant well, though he'd been harping on Shane and me taking over the business. That wasn't in my cards, and I guessed he was aware of my thought process even though I'd never described it to him. There was no point. I would go into the NFL, which I knew he supported. But the company was something he'd dreamed of handing down to us. Shane and I would work things out with Grandad's business. If he didn't want to run it, we would find someone who could on our behalf.

"What I'm leaving you and your brother is a legacy, and I expect the business to prosper when I turn it over to you boys."

My head throbbed, as did the bruises from where Jake had managed to tag me. I needed him to get on with it so that I could crash. We had a long run in the morning before practice.

"I've come to find out about a situation you've found yourself in." His bushy eyebrows lowered, and I swear steam came out of his nose.

"What are you talking about?" *School? Aspen? The baby? Fighting? The problems between Shane and me?* The list was lengthy.

Grandad rested his elbows on the armrests and steepled his fingers. "I have an employee in human resources whose shares a mutual acquaintance with you."

"Okay." I had no idea where he was going with this and downed the rest of my water.

"Mark Reid."

I choked on the last sip at the mention of Aspen's father, spewing water everywhere. He knew. Shane had to have told him because I sure as hell had not.

"I see you know the young lady in question. Quite well, from what I've learned."

"I was going to tell you and Mom about Aspen."

"No need. But what you will do is throw next week's fight."

"What?" I wasn't even going to cover the topic of how he'd found out. "Why would I do that?"

"Why, indeed?" Grandad stood and went to the door, where he paused. "I lived through Linda's terrible choice of getting pregnant and destroying a young man's dreams, breaking her mother's heart, and ending with her taking her own life. I should have been more involved in my daughter's choices. I made mistakes with her, and I learned from them. If I'd acted, maybe she would still be around." He paused and swallowed. "And that brings me to my employee. I'm sure you wouldn't want anything to happen to Mr. Reid. Throw the fight, Phoenix. It's time to end things. I'll be watching."

Stunned, I just sat there as he waltzed out of my room as if he hadn't just issued an order to throw a fight and destroy my credibility, or he would take it out on Aspen's father. Grandad was an overbearing asshole and a lot of other things, but this was the first glimpse of ruthless and manipulative that I'd seen in him as ruthless and manipulative. It made Mom's rebellious nature that much easier to understand.

The more I thought about it and tried to find a way out of the impossible situation, I realized something unsettling. It was a test. Grandad wanted me to follow instructions to see if my pride was bigger than my loyalty. Not only that, but I wondered if he planned to place a bet against me. There was a lot of money to be made for anyone who knew the fight's outcome, especially if the favored contender didn't win. And after my fight tonight and how the odds had been stacked against me, I would be favored to win regardless of who the other opponent was.

I had never thrown a fight and couldn't believe I was even considering following his orders. I'd lost some, although not many, and I would have to take a beating to make it believable. Grandad made it clear that it wasn't my choice. Hell, he even knew about Aspen.

I wondered whether he really would fire her dad and take away Aspen's access to health insurance. I shoved my fingers through my hair and doubled over. Holy fuck, that was… evil. It gave me another window into my family. Mom's sister, aunt Linda, had taken her own life. The depression and miserable marriage were too much to bear. Part of me couldn't help but wonder if Grandad had also played a role in her unhappiness.

Mom was so strong and independent, refusing to accept any help unless it was for him to pay for something for us that she couldn't, and I suspected that was part of why she was working herself into an early grave—so he couldn't hold anything over her. Shane and I had always wondered. Grandad wasn't wealthy like Uncle Lucas, who was a billionaire, but he did all right.

But Grandad's money came with strings attached.

The money from the fight... I could bet big. We would need so much more if Aspen's access to health insurance was canceled. What I would have to do was becoming clearer. There wasn't a choice.

One thing that bothered me was that I didn't yet know who my opponent was. *Dammit, Shane.* I needed someone to talk to. I could only imagine what he would have thought about what I'd learned about Grandad or what he'd ordered me to do.

If Grandad was controlling me like a fucking puppet, it was possible that he had his mitts on who my opponent would be. Somehow, I didn't doubt it. In a fight, I'd never drawn Shane, Damon, or Cole. Maybe if it were one of them, the sting of cheating wouldn't be so severe. Or perhaps it would be worse.

CHAPTER TWENTY

ASPEN

Raw fear skated over my body in a volley of pins and needles. Several weeks had passed since that euphoric morning surfing with Riley, and I wished I could have another few hours on the water to resurrect that chill vibe.

But it wasn't meant to be. I'd made it through the weekend and to my midweek doctor's appointment—alone. Mom couldn't come, Regan was still out of state, and Phoenix couldn't be relied on. I didn't want him there, anyway.

But in that moment, I regretted not asking him to come. I should have because when the doc said there was a possibility of complications after the results of a blood test and they needed to do more testing, it took everything in me not to burst into tears.

I loved the little peanut—or alien, rather, as I was at four months—and the thought of something being wrong was too much to handle as I lay on the exam table. Warm gel spread over my stomach along with the gentle pressing of the ultrasound wand the doc wielded. The monitor was turned away from me while she took measurements. I needed to see what was going on and silently willed her to turn the screen toward me while I tried to pay attention to what she said.

"Is the test risky?"

"There is a small risk of miscarriage, but I think the test will be beneficial. I don't want you to worry about anything, though. The specialist I'm sending you to is excellent, and we'll wait until you're at fifteen weeks for this. Try not to stress. You'll be in good hands." The doc's voice was calm and soothing, but it didn't matter. Everything she said grated on my frayed nerves. "Does your family have a history of congenital disabilities? There was quite a bit missing in your patient history."

"I don't know. I'll have to talk to my parents and the baby's dad." Whether I wanted to or not, I had to. I would do anything to protect my baby.

I felt so helpless. I didn't know what questions to ask. The thought of something being wrong was terrifying, and I was already so in love with the baby that it felt like my whole world was crashing down on me, and I had no one to help me keep it together.

"That's a good idea. And I don't want you to stress about this. The likelihood of a problem is minimal. We will do what's best for you and the baby, no matter what. I don't want you to worry, Aspen. It won't hurt to have more information." She made a few more entries then paused to look at me, a soft smile curving her face. "Do you want to listen to the baby's heartbeat?"

"Yes." I tensed, desperate for signs that the little peanut was doing okay.

The doc turned up the volume, and a fast staccato filled the room. Tears leaked from the corners of my eyes, and I didn't try to stop them. Then she turned the screen to face me and pointed out the baby, who really did look like an alien. I was fascinated and couldn't tear my eyes from the screen. She pressed a few more buttons, and a printer whirled to life.

Then she handed me the black-and-white images, and I clung to them like the lifeline they were. *Everything is going to be all right. I promise, little angel.*

The rest of the appointment was a blur. At the reception desk, I made an appointment with the specialist for the amniocentesis and learned I would receive a call with instructions. There had been a cancelation, and they'd managed to squeeze me in the following week.

I left the office on shaky legs. Rain thundered down as I reached the lobby. Thunder cracked overhead, lighting up the cloudy, gray sky. I pushed through the heavy doors and stood under the overhang, knowing I would get drenched in seconds, having forgotten an umbrella, but there was no other option. I stepped out, and cold rain pelted me as I raced for the parking lot. Seconds later, thunder boomed so loudly that I felt it in my bones, and the hairs on my arms stood from the charged air.

Soaked, I slammed my car door shut and shivered. I turned the key and breathed a sigh of relief as the engine turned over. I waited for the car to warm enough to blast hot air through the vents directed at me. The weather was intense. The wind pushed the rain diagonally, and ferocious pings knocked against my car. Visibility sucked, and I cranked the windshield wipers to high, very glad the distance to my dorm wasn't too far.

I needed to call Mom, but that would have to wait. She wouldn't be able to hear me over the storm. It was loud inside my car, and even the slightest driving distraction would be dangerous. As I carefully pulled into traffic, driving at an alarmingly slow pace, I couldn't stop thinking about what Mom would say, if anything. She'd been supportive overall, but her disappointment was tangible. Dad was worse. We still weren't on speaking terms, not really. Every time I called, he somehow managed to be busy or had to get off the phone after a question or two.

I didn't think I'd ever felt so alone.

Mom's sister, Aunt Sylvia, didn't have any kids and lived in Australia. We had minimal contact with her aside from birthday cards. Dad came from a big family of six brothers and sisters. He was the baby, with a nine-year gap between the last one and him. None of them were close, and he rarely spoke to them. I doubted that either of them would know their full family history of congenital birth defects.

I made it home, parked, dashed into my dorm, grabbed my bathroom stuff from my room, and went straight into a hot shower. I didn't think the day could get any worse. At least my roommate wasn't there. I didn't think I could handle pretending everything was okay.

I could call Max, but first, I needed to face Mom and Dad. In my warmest pajamas, I burrowed under a blanket and called them. My gut clenched and rolled with nerves that I suspected would be with me until the results of the amnio came in.

"Aspen." Mom sounded breathless again. "Everything all right?"

"Yeah." Sort of. "Are you good?"

"Just running in from the garage. It's really coming down out there. How's school going?"

"School's easy. It's the last thing on my mind lately."

"Aspen." She had that scolding tone.

I leaned back against the wall, tucking the pink comforter Regan had made for me tighter around me.

"School is the most important thing. You know I would have liked to finish. Don't throw this opportunity away."

I rolled my eyes. It was the same story and argument that had been shouted in our house for as long as I could remember. "I have all A's. School isn't a problem."

"Oh. Well, that's good."

It hurt that she didn't ask about the baby or how I felt, especially since she was supposed to go to the doctor with me. At the beginning, both of my parents had made it clear that they didn't approve of the situation I'd found myself in and had even given me information for abortion clinics. I couldn't lie and pretend that it hadn't crossed my mind. And if I'd gotten pregnant in high school, I probably would have made that hard choice to end the pregnancy. But… I was old enough, and I already loved the baby. I'd made up my mind, even if no one else would help.

That wasn't true. I knew my sister would. And Phoenix was committed to being there for the baby, even though I didn't see a lot of follow-through beyond those envelopes of money. I guessed we would see later, which also worried me.

I chose to ignore her negativity. "Mom, do we have any family history of congenital disabilities?"

"No. Why are you asking?"

"The doctor wants to do an amniocentesis test, and she mentioned I should ask about our family history. Do you know about Dad's side?"

"Please. Like that man shares anything with me? You'll have to ask him."

I felt sick and said nothing.

"Have you told Phoenix about the test yet?"

"No. He's been busy with football and school. We haven't had time to talk, and I didn't want to do it over the phone." Or at all. Mom didn't know the truth about what Phoenix and I were to each other. Fake dating was something we upheld to family and around school. But anyone near us had to have heard our fights. They were epic.

"Well, you need to make the time for that, Aspen. It's important."

"I know." Her voice was heavy with disapproval, and I didn't know why she couldn't cut me a break. She'd gone to a doctor's appointment with me and had been supportive, but then there were those times when her true feelings came through loud and clear. She hadn't said it yet, but I got the impression that she had zero interest in being a grandmother. "Can you talk to Dad and see if there's any history on his side?"

"You should be the one doing that, but," a loud sigh sounded through the speaker, "I'll ask him."

"Thanks, Mom. I've got to get some homework done. I'll talk to you soon."

We hung up, and my anxiety amped back up as I scrolled through my contacts. A fat tear rolled down my cheek as I paused on Phoenix's name.

I had to tell him.

CHAPTER TWENTY-ONE

PHOENIX

In a haze, I managed to make it to Tuesday, which was a miracle in itself. My grandad's dictate about the fight and the unspoken threat to her dad and to the health insurance Aspen needed had sucker punched me more than once and left me reeling.

My lifeline through it all was football, the one thing he hadn't threatened. He could have. I was only too aware of that because he knew about the underground fights and my participation in them. It was career-ending knowledge, and the man I'd thought I could trust had proven me wrong.

If I was to go through with the fight, I swore it would be the last one. My next goal would be to do everything in my power to get drafted early. This year was out because I had missed a few games, but maybe next year could work. I couldn't leave anything to fate again—not Aspen and the baby, not my career, or even my brother or Mom's well-being. If he was capable of doing that to me, I shuddered to think what he would do—or had done—to them.

Tired of being alone in my room, I leaned against the

kitchen counter in the football house. Damon and Cole walked in, and some other guys left for dinner at the cafeteria.

"How's it going?" Cole opened the fridge and grabbed an apple.

He'd been around less between football, classes, and Riley's diving meets. Damon had been busy, too, off doing his own thing with Sky. I loved college, but it was a big change.

"Good. You going to be around after practice tomorrow? I wanted to go over tape."

"Yeah, that sounds good." Cole hitched his bag higher on his shoulder. "I've got to get a paper written. Will you guys be around later?"

"I'm sleeping at Sky's. Her roommate isn't there tonight." Damon bowed out. "I'll see you both later. I just needed to grab a few things. But tomorrow is good. Count me in."

My phone rang as they both exited the kitchen. Aspen's photo lit up the screen, and I answered, my gut instantly tightening. She rarely reached out, and whenever she did, it made me worry that something was wrong with the baby.

"Phoenix?" Her voice was high-pitched and tight.

"Hey, everything okay?" I straightened from the counter, ready to book out of there if she needed me.

"I need to talk to you. Can you meet me at the diner?"

"When?"

"Now."

I said I would and left in a rush. There hadn't been one time we'd met at the diner without all hell breaking loose, and I expected nothing less this time. It was obvious by her tone of voice that something was wrong.

I drove instead of walked, so it didn't take long. When I arrived, Aspen was in a booth with a glass of water. I slid in on the opposite side as people moved around us. The place was packed, per usual.

"Okay, I'm here. Tell me what's wrong."

Big blue eyes locked onto mine, and a chill skated down my spine. She looked haunted, forlorn. I was used to her either being mad or living in her free-spirit surfer vibe. This, I didn't like. But I waited until she was ready.

She took a deep breath then released it slowly. "The doctor wants to run some additional tests. I'm supposed to ask you if your family has any history of congenital disabilities."

I grabbed one of her hands, needing the lifeline. "Not that I know of. What tests?"

Her fingers tightened on mine, and I caught the slight tremor that ran through them. Then she told me about the test and the long fucking needle that would be inserted into her belly to take some of the amniotic fluid. I didn't like the sound of it and planned to talk to Mom no matter what Grandad said about *him* keeping an eye on things, which usually meant "don't bother your mother with your petty problems."

I wanted to fix things for her, but I felt lost. "Do you need more money? I can get you more."

She snatched her hand back, and that permanent scowl, the one that seemed to be present whenever I was around, returned.

"I don't need money. I'm on my dad's insurance until I'm twenty-six."

"I'm sorry. I don't know what to do to help."

A tiny bit of her anger seemed to subside as the red that'd infused her cheeks faded. She took a sip of water, and I kept my mouth shut, not wanting to piss her off even more. But when she stood and left without another word, I knew how badly I'd screwed up. I couldn't get anything right with her.

I chased after her, clipping one of the servers in the shoulder, and had to stop to help her steady her tray. If I hadn't, her four top would have been drenched. Apologizing, I darted out, avoiding running into anyone else.

It was chilly outside, and a stiff breeze gave the door some resistance as I went through it. The sidewalk was busy, as it was after work and dinnertime. That area was constantly congested. I craned my neck, checking both directions until I spotted her blond head through a break in the foot traffic.

I caught up with her and nudged her to the side, so the crowd shifted around us. We couldn't leave things like that, with me in the dark and her furious.

"When's the test?"

"Friday, early afternoon."

I had a game Friday night, but I could make both. I had to. "Text me the address and time, and I'll be there."

CHAPTER TWENTY-TWO

ASPEN

I should have known that Phoenix wouldn't bother to show up for the amniocentesis, even though he'd promised. Yeah, it was Friday, and a couple of days had passed since I told him, but he should've remembered. He was an unreliable asshole, not father material at all.

I regretted that second glass of water so hard as I crossed my legs, waiting in a chair close to the door where I would be called back. I was supposed to drink so much to move my bladder out of the way of the needle's entry. I couldn't even think about that. *And screw you, Phoenix.* I shouldn't have been surprised that he was a no-show.

A few others were in the room with swollen stomachs and their partners right by their sides. Not me. Nope. I was alone. *Better get used to it.*

I dropped my face into my hands, bending at my waist, trying to get rid of the nerves that were utterly out of control. I did what I always did when things were too much to deal with and pictured the ocean, connecting to peaceful blue waters then the perfect wave, that feeling of catching it, jumping to my feet, and the perfect release of endorphins and adrenaline. Worry and pain slipped away. There was only me and the ocean as I rode that wave to the shore.

It was where I belonged, where I felt the happiest. I took a deep breath, and on its release, I sat back and opened my eyes. The room seemed smaller, as if someone was sucking up all the presence. My skin prickled with awareness, and in walked Phoenix. Heads turned.

I couldn't blame them. Mine turned, too, when he was near. Well over six feet tall, athletic, and muscular, he naturally drew attention. But even beyond his size, his looks kept people's focus. He was gorgeous, sexy, and impossible not to want.

I hated that he affected me so much. My defenses rocketed back up, and any peace I'd gained from the beach meditation evaporated.

He said nothing as he took the seat next to me and grabbed my hand. Tingles shot up my arm at the contact, but I didn't let go. I… needed him there, which was hard to admit.

"Are you worried?" He sounded subdued.

My jaw clenched. "Of course, I'm worried."

He nodded, and I observed him from the corner of my eye, not ready to fully acknowledge him for being late. Lines bracketed his mouth, and he stared straight ahead. He appeared relaxed. I shifted slightly for a closer look. He wasn't. His body was tense, his muscles rock-hard and flexed. It made me feel better and erased some of my annoyance about how he hadn't been on time.

Then I glanced at the clock, and all the anger returned. "You would have missed the appointment if the technician had been on time." I yanked my hand away and crossed my arms over my chest. Jerk. I would have to do this by myself, scared and alone. I shook my head. It was something I needed to get used to.

"I'm sorry. I had a prior commitment."

"More important than this?" He said nothing, and even though I'd never hit anyone, I wanted to slap the hell out of his beautiful face.

God, I was generally a very happy, laid-back person. I surfed and painted. Aside from the shit show of living with my parents before coming here, my life had been relaxed. They were the ones that needed so much. I hadn't. I had been content with the art supplies that I made enough money by waitressing in high school to purchase, usually, and Regan made many of our clothes.

Lately, I was on a roller coaster of emotions and anger. It sucked. And Phoenix's lack of reliability was tipping me over the edge of crazy. I didn't like it.

He turned to face me. "I didn't know your dad worked at Bennett Property Management for my grandad."

What the hell? Defensive. That was me. But really—he was bringing that up to remind me he was the fancy rich guy and my family was barely hanging on. I knew it.

"Good thing about the insurance."

I let my head fall back and clamped my mouth even tighter before I laid into him because it seemed like he'd just thrown in my face how his family provided the insurance for my dad. The same insurance I was using for the pregnancy. Nope. I couldn't do it. "What the hell is that supposed to mean?" I hissed as quietly as possible because we were getting way too much attention from the other patients waiting to be called back.

His brows furrowed, and the brackets around his mouth deepened as a storm brewed in his silver eyes. "It doesn't mean anything, Aspen. I didn't know your dad worked for my grandad. That's it. I was worried about the insurance."

Bullshit. And I was going to tell him that, but the door opened, and my name was called. I stood on shaky legs, barely looking at him. He could come or not. I didn't care.

The technician, who was female and clearly fixated on

Phoenix, led me back to the room then instructed me to get on the exam table. It was raised slightly so that my head was elevated.

She ignored me and flirted, touching his arm then showing him where to sit, which was in the chair beside me, the pregnant one. The only saving grace was that he'd severed the contact immediately and shifted his focus to me, ignoring her until she told him to have a seat. It didn't change how angry I was, but it helped.

The lighting in the small room was dim, and I appreciated that so much. Scattered around were several instruments whose function I couldn't identify and two monitors. I assumed those would be where we watched the baby. My doc said they would be doing an ultrasound at the same time. The doc, an older man with salt-and-pepper hair and a kind smile, came in, and I relaxed a tiny bit.

"I'm Dr. Harrison. And you're Aspen Reid?"

"Yes." I felt shaky. The pressure on my bladder was intense. I wasn't even sure I could make it through the test without peeing myself. My cheeks flamed at that unpleasant thought.

Phoenix noticed and frowned.

Whatever. He could think anything he wanted.

Dr. Harrison shook Phoenix's hand. "Mr. Reid?"

"Phoenix Bennett, but I'm the baby's father."

Interesting. I was slightly fascinated by his reaction because it was open and honest. He was claiming rights. Part of me loved it, and the other half… well, the jury was still out.

The same annoying technician entered, and Phoenix turned away from her, taking my hand in his instead. I allowed it only because of her. I glared, and she caught it. So did the doc. Good. Maybe he would have words with her later.

"I've been informed that you finished your second glass of water a half hour ago, Aspen?"

"Yes." And we needed to hurry along.

"What we're going to do is have a look at your baby with the ultrasound. Then you'll feel some pressure and a pinch of pain from the needle while I extract a small amount of the amniotic fluid. I don't want you to worry. Everything will be fine, and we'll all be watching where your baby is in relation to the needle. How are you doing so far?"

"Fine."

"Wanting to get this over with?" He chuckled, and I grinned.

"Very much so."

"Okay." He nodded to the tech, and she adjusted my clothing to expose my stomach and the tiny baby bump forming.

Phoenix's hand spasmed in mine, and I turned to catch his stunned expression. Then it hit me. He hadn't seen the slight change in my body because I hadn't been wearing tight clothing for a couple of weeks.

It made things more real.

The doc squirted warm gel on my stomach then pressed the wand against my belly, moving it around to get all the angles he needed of the little alien growing inside me.

"Hold it here, Becca."

She went around to his side and did as he asked. Dr. Harrison picked up a large needle from the tray next to him, and my eyes widened.

"Holy shit."

Phoenix had the right to say that. I wanted to hop off the table and run. Instead, I tightened my grip on his hand. He was my lifeline, whether he wanted to be or not.

"You'll feel a small pinch and pressure." Dr. Harrison said. "It's important that you don't move."

"Okay." I wouldn't risk anything happening to the baby, so I would do as he said and be a statue. Phoenix scooted closer, and both of us locked onto the monitor. *Please, little baby, don't move.*

The doc positioned the needle then inserted it into my stomach at an angle. I gasped then whimpered, squeezing the hell out of Phoenix's hand. We could see the needle inside me on the monitor. The pressure was intense, and lightheadedness swirled, but I blinked away the black dots on the edge of my vision.

Then it was over. The pain left, but not the pressure from my bladder. "Can I get up and use the bathroom?"

"Yes, of course."

Phoenix helped me stand and walked me to the bathroom door. "I've got it." I released him and went inside by myself, locking the door then shoving my leggings down as quickly as possible. I fell onto the toilet seat, thankful I didn't pee all over myself. After washing my hands, I went back into the room.

But I felt sick. "I think I'm going to throw up."

"Have a seat, Aspen." Dr. Harrison's voice sounded far off.

Phoenix guided me to the chair, but I lost my grip on the world around me, and everything went dark.

"Mommy, let's go."

Wild blond curls dance in the wind, and a tiny hand brushes them out of her eyes. She has the face of an angel. A masculine roar sounds, and my little girl is swooped up in muscular, tatted arms. Squeals of laughter ring over the hypnotic roll of waves as they break along the shore.

I push up from my towel, brush off the sand, and join them as Phoenix flies her like an airplane to the water. The sun beats down on us, and carefree laughter spills from my lips. We're at my favorite place, and I'm spending the day with my family. I love everything about this afternoon.

Phoenix turns, our laughing little girl secure in his arms as he calls for me to join them, and I run over hot sand to the lapping waves to do just that. The foamy water tickles my skin as I wade in after them, not mistaking the spark of heat in those unusual silver eyes of his. Then his muscular arms sweep me against his side, and our little angel's tiny hands reach for me too. It is the best kind of day.

"Aspen!"

The bright, warm day morphed into a dim examination room, but I reached for my little girl and him, not wanting our time together to end. A sense of panic and anxiety filtered in as they faded away. I moaned as they disappeared, and a bitter smell assaulted my senses.

With a slow blink, Phoenix's stricken features swam before my eyes. I had to open and close them a few more times to bring him into sharp focus. He bent before me, both my hands in his. He looked scared. "What happened?"

"Here, drink this." The doctor pressed an orange juice into my hand, which Phoenix seemed reluctant to release.

I took a few sips, and the doc moved back. Phoenix did not.

"Your blood pressure dropped, and you passed out." Dr. Harrison explained, "It sometimes happens after emptying your bladder and the high-stress situation. Nothing to worry about."

Becca busied herself with organizing the room, probably for the next patient. The doctor waited patiently for me to finish the drink. I handed the empty cup to Phoenix.

"How are you feeling?" the doc asked.

"I'm fine." A muscle jumped along Phoenix's clenched jaw, and I watched it in fascination, more embarrassed I'd passed out than anything.

"The results will be sent to your doctor's office in two weeks. Nothing strenuous for the next twenty-four hours. That includes lifting anything over twenty pounds. Try to keep your mind off the test results in the meantime. And if you have any questions, please call."

"Thank you."

Phoenix stood and walked to the door with the doctor. He spoke to him, but I couldn't hear what he said. Then he was at my side, helping me stand. I didn't need him to, but I let him because that experience had been over the top. I wasn't going to touch on the vision I'd had while passed out. I'd seen her twice.

Her.

I held Phoenix's gaze as he came back to me. He helped me to my feet, and I moved as if in a daze, surprised when we were outside and standing by my car. I couldn't hold it in anymore. I had to tell him. "We're having a girl."

"What? How do you know?"

"I just do." I wanted to share more, but something held me back. I wasn't ready to tell him I'd seen her. Not yet. Before he could ask anything else, I changed the subject. "So what happened in there? I mean, I know I passed out, but you looked pretty freaked out."

He ran a hand over his face and looked to the cloudy sky as if there were answers. "I was. You lost all the color in your face and just fell."

"I don't feel sore." *Had I hit my head?*

"I caught you, and the doc told me to put you in the chair. Then they took out smelling salts. They set the tiny tube under your nose, but you didn't wake up. It was about a full minute until you did."

"I heard you."

"Yeah, I was shouting your name. I'm surprised they didn't kick me out for disturbing the other patients."

I was confused but didn't want to analyze anything. "I'm pretty tired. I think I'm going to go home and get some rest."

"I'm not sure you should drive yourself. I can take you back."

"No." Then I wouldn't have my car. Or he would come in with me, and I didn't trust myself because falling asleep in his arms was what I wanted more than anything. The one-hundred-eighty-degree shift of emotions with him today was too much, and I felt way too vulnerable. "I'm fine. And I'll call you when I get the test results."

His phone rang, and when he pulled it out and looked at the screen, he swore. I took that as my cue to get in the car. His eyes flicked to mine once more before he took off toward his SUV.

I was right not to give in to him. As always, he left. And

despite the dream or vision or whatever it was, the truth was that he wouldn't be there for me—for us.

CHAPTER TWENTY-THREE

PHOENIX

Holy shit, that was fucking insane. They stuck a needle as long as my forearm into Aspen's stomach, and she took it like a badass. Maybe Grandad should have bet on her. I had a feeling she would put him in his place without even breaking a sweat.

I wasn't handling things with him very well. But he was family... he'd been there for Shane and me. Even if I didn't agree —at all—with his current manipulative methods, I didn't see any other way out. Once I was in the NFL, I wouldn't have to rely on him for anything. His visit had highlighted the dark secrets in our family and that what I thought I knew was likely wrong.

After parking, I hurried inside to grab some food before leaving for the game. Shane was coming out of the kitchen, and we almost collided.

"You look like shit."

He scowled, only accenting how tired he appeared with the same heavy circles under his eyes like what Mom always had. "You don't look much better."

I could only imagine what I looked like. That shit with Aspen had been insane.

Shane just stood there, not saying a word, and I pulled myself from my head. He was finally here, not running off to somewhere else, and for once, I didn't want to argue with him. Things were already fucked beyond repair. I needed my brother back.

"You going to the game?" I shouldn't have had to ask. Football was a huge part of our lives, and there simply was no missing games or practices unless we physically couldn't participate.

"What kind of question is that?" he snapped. "Of course I'm going."

I could tell we were going to come to blows if I didn't defuse the energy. I took a step back and a deep breath and deliberately relaxed my posture. "I have no idea what's going on with you, man. You're here for a few minutes and then gone. You don't say where you are or who you're with, so I'm left guessing. And I need to talk to you." He was completely clueless about what was going on in my life. "The only thing that makes sense to me is that you're back with Tracey. Because your absence..." I didn't want to say the rest. He knew what school was like for me, and he'd fucking bailed. But I went for it. "You not being here has made shit really hard for me, dude."

"And the shit you've done hasn't been hard on me?" He blinked then looked away. "Dammit, Phoenix. It's not about Tracey." He scowled. "Well, it was before, but that's not it anymore."

"I'm sorry." *Fuck.* I linked my hands behind my neck and looked to the ceiling. Nothing was fixed. I could still feel the distance like a wall between us. "School is kicking my ass, and I'm worried about football. I needed your help."

"I... I'm equally as concerned about my scholarship and the extra money I have to pay... Not everyone got a full ride like you did. And I can't take on your struggles too." An angry breath crashed between us as he brushed past me, heading for the door. "I've just got a lot going on. I'll see you at the field."

I got an orange from the fridge and slammed the door shut, causing things to rattle dangerously inside. I didn't have time for anything else. On the way out, I passed Damon.

"What was that about? I just saw Shane, and he has that same pissed-off expression." He pointed at me. "You two fighting again?"

"How could we? He doesn't stay around long enough to have an actual conversation." I was furious with my brother, but most of all, I missed him. And I hadn't even gotten a chance to ask him if he'd had any weird encounters with Grandad.

"He hasn't been around all that much, but I haven't been worried because the few times I see him on campus he's been with a girl."

That was news. "Did you ask him about her?" Could he have finally moved past the crap with Tracey for real?

"No. Since he hasn't brought her around the football house, I assumed they weren't serious, or not yet. Maybe I was wrong?"

Damon looked like he was expecting me to say more about Shane. I had nothing. The girl was news to me. And after finding out my brother was stressed about school, too, I felt bad that I hadn't seen things from his perspective. I was still mad at him... we had shit to work through. And I hoped we could.

I glanced at the time on the microwave. Shit, we had to get a move on, or Coach would hand us our asses. "Is Cole already at the stadium?"

"Yeah. I'll see you there."

Damon took off, and I went to my SUV, climbed in, and left for the stadium. The ride gave me time to think. Things were getting real with Aspen's pregnancy. Seeing the baby... I'd never experienced feelings like that before, and every protective and possessive instinct roared to life. In that moment, for as corny as it was to say, everything changed.

Then it hit me like a freight train. I should have called her and made sure she was all right after the test. I should have asked what I could do. But I had been weak and stupid and selfish. I knew that to be strong, I had to let myself be vulnerable with her. I was an idiot for acting like I didn't care when I did. I was a fool for not letting her help me with my stupid homework. We needed to lean on each other.

But that almost conversation with Shane had left me reeling in another direction. My life was fucked up, and I was fucked up. On the field, I could let it all go. I needed football like my next breath, but I needed Aspen too. I just didn't know how to tell her that.

I would call her soon. I just hoped it wasn't too late. She'd looked furious when I showed up late to the doctor. Maybe if I'd just told her what was going on... but then again, she had enough on her plate, and I didn't need to add to that. I shook my head and tapped the steering wheel. Enough of that for the time being. I had work to do.

Traffic was already heavy, so I took the back roads to the parking lot for players and employees.

I let myself sift through whatever was on my mind in that moment, because as soon as I hit that locker room—football would be the only thing taking up any headspace.

Where I struggled in school or reading or with relationships, I excelled on the gridiron. I could read the playbook without difficulty, and the gratitude I felt for football astounded me. It was in my blood—the stress and worry dropped off with each step until my senses were filled with the turf, the lines, the stands, the hallway to the locker room, the sounds of the other players getting pumped for the game. The perfect snap, the feeling of the ball in my hand, and letting it soar through the air to the intended target made everything else go away.

The warmth that blanketed me when I entered the locker room made my tight muscles relax. Players were in various stages of undress, getting taped up, stretching, or collaborating with teammates and coaches.

Each of us had a unique pregame ritual. Damon stretched with headphones in, while Shane fed on the chaos and noise, preferring not to wear them. Cole could be found participating in several conversations with teammates and coaches.

There were a few shouts and some laughter. Expectant energy crackled through the space. Guys walked around or stretched to limber up their muscles and tendons. Speeches from Coach would come later. With a towel around my neck and my eyes closed, I systematically dismissed everything to focus on the game—what I could see happening. Perfect spirals dropping into the hands of my intended targets.

I visualized plays and outcomes and ended with feeling the rush of victory. Only then did I open my eyes and let the sounds and sights filter back into awareness, hyper-focused and charged for what would happen on that field.

My eyes snapped open, ready to lead the team.

I would do whatever was necessary to protect Aspen and our baby. That was my last thought as I entered the tunnel with my teammates, anticipation and adrenaline filling me as the stadium roared at our entrance. My problems faded. My drive was absolute, and nothing distracted me. I could compartmentalize and get to work.

CHAPTER TWENTY-FOUR

ASPEN

Worry churned in my stomach, and it was only Saturday. I knew the next two weeks of waiting for the test results would be the longest moments of my life, even longer than the three minutes it had taken for the test to tell me I was pregnant. Living with the what-if fear was driving me crazy.

And I shouldn't have been surprised, but I hadn't heard from Phoenix, either, and I felt mildly disappointed. There had been a game last night after the test, so I kind of understood. Maybe. I wished I could just get over it and over him, but a constant reminder of him was growing in my belly.

I needed a distraction, and Max could usually provide that.

I went up to his room and knocked. I'd texted to see if he was around, but he hadn't answered. Maybe he'd gone out. I would give it another—

The door opened, and Max stood there with messy hair, looking like he'd just woken up or... A noise sounded behind him. Nope, not sleeping. He had company.

But I didn't want to be alone, and he must have sensed that because he held the door open. I walked under his arm and into his room.

I stopped short at the sight of a shirtless, scrawny Elias Kincaid sprawled out on Max's bed, and a half-empty bottle of Patron balanced on the flat bedpost. At least he had most of his clothes on. I still wasn't a fan. We'd seen each other around campus, had one class together, and had met at Phoenix's fight. We rubbed each other the wrong way, and I'd overheard from the group he hung out with one day that he was a mean drunk. He was arrogant and overly flamboyant in a look-at-me-I-need-attention sort of way. I was pretty sure we shared that instant I-don't-like-you vibe.

Max remained over by the door as I glanced between them. Max was calm, resolved, but Elias's expression turned stormy at the interruption as he scowled at Max then zeroed in on me.

"Oh, surprise, surprise. If it isn't the preggo surfer chick crashing our date." Elias sneered.

The door closed behind me, and Max came to stand at my side. "Elias, that's enough. Aspen's my friend. Be nice."

Elias cackled. There was no other word for his fake, high-pitched laugh. "That is me being nice." He swung his legs over the edge of the bed. "If I were being nasty, I would have said, 'way to go on getting knocked up by the dumb one. Good thing he's pretty to look at because that's all you'll get when that baby pops out.'"

"You're an ass. And Phoenix isn't dumb."

Elias rolled his eyes. "Please. I went to high school with him. He was in a group who called themselves—I kid you not—'the Elite.' They thought they were everything, and the stupid sheep in that school treated them like gods. They weren't"—he shrugged one thin shoulder—"and I thought the new girl our last year at the academy would put at least one of them in their place."

He was talking about Riley, and my anger notched up another degree.

"But she fell under their spell just like the rest of them."

"You sound delusional with a strong side of jealousy."

"Oh please, little punt bunny." Elias pouted his lower lip in some sort of exaggerated, sarcastic gesture.

"Elias," Max snapped, his body tense beside me. "What's your problem?"

Elias ignored him, and I readied myself for the attack his predatory gleam indicated, with a nice little dig of my own. "Closet-obsessed-fan."

"Aspen," Max growled, shifting so he stood almost between us, ready to throw out arms to keep us from leaping at each other with claws bared.

"And you're an opportunist." Elias made a point to stare at my belly. "Good luck landing him. I hear someone prettier has his eye."

"Elias, please," Max said, crossing his arms, disgust pulling his mouth into a hard slash. We both continued to ignore him as we traded epithets. "You're both being horrible."

Fucking Jillian. "Then you're dumber than I thought." I leaned closer, only about two feet separating me from smacking Elias in the head. "Phoenix and I are dating. He told Jillian to fuck off."

"I see you're just as stupid as the dumb one. My friend Jillian is NFL-wife material. While you're"—an ugly sneer consumed his face— "you."

A dark laugh spilled from my lips. "Say what you want about me. I don't care. I'm comfortable with how intelligent I am. But Phoenix? You've got him all wrong, little closet fan."

Elias tsked. "I had the misfortune of having the pretty one in lit class senior year at HVA. He can barely read. Better hope you can, or your little bambino doesn't stand a chance of making it through life on more than looks."

I had no idea what he was talking about, but I couldn't let him get away with how insulting he was. "You're a hateful queen. Is that because you have a thing for Phoenix but he didn't return your interest? Tearing someone down makes you feel better?"

"Hardly." His eyelid twitched. "I just call it like I see it."

I shook. I was so angry. Max shifted on his feet, looking as if he didn't know who to defend. My anger spilled onto my friend for associating with Elias. Whatever. I could hold my own ground.

"Do you have any idea what it takes to be a quarterback? It takes leadership, a keen analytical sense, a solid understanding of the plays, and the ability to make quick decisions based on what you see on the field before the ball is snapped and immediately after. And from everything I've seen and read about Phoenix, he's a prodigy out there." I was glad I'd done that football research.

"He must have help because the dumb bunny can't read." Elias delivered with an upward tilt of his chin.

He was such a hateful person. I had no idea what Max saw in him. I turned to my friend. "I liked Joel better. Is this a one-and-done hookup? Because I feel like I'm wasting my breath here."

"You bitch!" Elias grabbed his shirt and stormed out of the room, knocking me in the shoulder on his way out. Max trailed behind him.

I couldn't believe this. I was so angry and then lightheaded. I went to the desk chair and sat, taking a few deep breaths until I felt better.

A few minutes later, I was back to normal when the door opened and Max came back into his room alone. "Well, that was nice while it lasted."

I chortled, disgusted that Max had wasted one minute of his time with that jerk. "Elias is all drama and such an asshole. Did you hear how he just talked to me? You can do better."

Max stayed by the door and remained quiet. I didn't say anything else, waiting for him to agree. He had to have seen how bad Elias was. The guy was toxic.

"You're one to talk."

"What?" *Did I hear that correctly?*

He raked his hands through his disheveled dark hair, making it stand up at odd angles, then went to the opposite side of the room on stiff legs and leaned against the wall. Crossing his arms, he leveled me with a cool look. "Everything is always about you."

Even though his voice was quiet, I felt the power of his words as if he'd slapped me. I had no comeback. Maybe I was wrong—not for defending myself or Phoenix, but for crashing his date and not caring.

"It always is, Aspen." Still, his voice was low and even-toned. "I have a life, too, not that you ask me about what's going on. The world hasn't stopped for everyone else just because you got with the hot football god, banged his pretty little brain out, and got yourself knocked up."

I sucked in a breath, blinking away tears. "What the hell, Max?" On shaky feet, I stood, shocked that he thought that about me.

"I liked Elias."

Oh wow, okay. But he needed to open his eyes. That guy was an asshole who clearly hated me. If Max stayed with him, I was sure the time would come when he had to make a choice, and I was fairly certain I wouldn't be the one to push an ultimatum. I stepped toward the door and rested my hand on the handle. I didn't open it, sensing he had more to say, even if I didn't want to hear what that was.

"He wasn't an asshole to me. And it's not for you to decide."

I jerked my head down in a nod, unable to say that I was sorry. I was, but only for the hurt I'd caused. I left quietly, making sure the door didn't slam behind me. Then I was in my room, not remembering the walk to get there.

I toed off my shoes and changed into my most comfy pajamas. Usually, Max was the guy I would call after a shitty argument. But that one had been with him, and I had no one left. Tears slid down my cheeks, dampening my pillowcase. Was I really so selfish that I never asked how Max was doing or took an interest in his life? Had I made everything about me?

The walls felt like they were closing in around me. People left the dorms or came in, their muted voices filtering through the door or window, and I'd never felt more alone in my life.

CHAPTER TWENTY-FIVE

PHOENIX

I wished I could go back to Friday night's game, but I couldn't, so I spent quite a bit of time just lying in bed and staring at the ceiling.

Saturday had dawned with a cloud of apprehension. I saw no way out of what I had to do that night. I still didn't understand why Grandad had demanded that I throw the fight. I saw no legitimate reason for it.

It was almost time to leave, and as usual, Shane wasn't home. If I'd ever needed him, it was the time. Throwing a game or a fight or any kind of cheating really didn't sit right with me. I'd never done that before. It sure as fuck would have been nice to know why Grandad had threatened me with Aspen's dad's job and her health insurance to get me to do it. Because there had to have been a reason aside from testing my loyalty to do as I was told.

I needed to talk to Shane about it. We were brothers, twins. We'd shared a womb, for fuck's sake.

All I could do was suck it up and get the fight over with. I glanced around the room one last time, stalling. Shane's half looked like a tornado'd hit it, except for his bed, which was sort of made and barely slept in. I had no idea where my brother had been crashing.

I kept my clothes in the laundry hamper, not all over the floor, chair, and bed. We'd always been opposites in organizational skills. His mess should have been a hindrance, but it wasn't. He didn't struggle with school, and the chaos of his surroundings never bothered him. I'd always felt out of control because of how hard it was to read, so I tried my best with the things I could regulate, like keeping my room and everything else in my life orderly.

I was screwing up big time with Aspen. In spite of my little epiphany the night before, I still hadn't called her. *I'll do better.* I just had to make it through a shit show of a fight.

I didn't know who my opponent would be. And part of me wondered if Grandad had a sick sense of humor and it would be Shane.

Keys in hand, I went to the door but stopped short when it opened. I blinked twice just to make sure I didn't imagine Shane. "Hey, where've you been?" I couldn't stop the question from spilling out.

He shrugged then dropped his gym bag on the floor, not looking at me once. There was something off about him. "Around. Just busy." He riffled through a pile of clothes until he found whatever he needed. Then he unzipped the bag and stuffed a few things inside.

Two defensive ends walked past our room. I waved, acknowledging them as they went down the hall. It was Sunday night, and most were studying or going to the fights.

I watched Shane fidget, something he didn't often do unless he was worried. He was acting shifty. Maybe trying to talk to him was a bad idea.

He leaned against his desk and crossed his arms over his chest. "Damon said you have a tutor. How's that going?"

I shrugged, a small smirk playing at the corners of my

mouth. Aspen had been fierce, and once I got over myself, I liked her helping me instead of Noel. Listening to her voice and having her so close for the short time we had to study when I wasn't training had turned out to be my favorite part of the day. "Aspen kicked her out. She's reading the chapters to me now." I was still mad at him for essentially ghosting me with school, but it was nice that he was home and talking longer than the few seconds it took him to grab clothes.

Shane threaded his hands behind his neck and tilted his head back. "Look… There's just been some stuff going on, and… I've got to go, but we should talk later."

"I have a fight. Don't you?" It irritated me that I didn't even know. Damon wasn't scheduled tonight and wasn't going to do it anymore. Cole had already stopped. It was just Shane and me, but maybe he'd pulled out too. I wouldn't know, as he never fucking talked to me anymore. I didn't move from where I'd stopped. My feet had grown roots. "Shane?"

"Oh, no. I'm not fighting tonight. But I'll be there, and we'll talk after." He grabbed his bag. "Later."

I got a text with the new location and waited a minute to calm down before heading out myself. My stomach was a mass of nerves.

I hated having my final fight in the underground ring end with an obvious loss, but I had no other choice.

I didn't feel comfortable talking to Shane about Grandad, even though part of me wished I'd brought it up. Maybe Shane was in on it. Even thinking that felt like a betrayal, but I was getting such weird vibes from my brother that anything was possible.

When I got to the warehouse, deep in one of the seedy areas of town, I flipped my hood up and kept my head down. I rapped my fist against the metal door until the usual bouncer, Tom, opened it. He was enormous and could have been a defensive lineman, but he wasn't, and I didn't care to find out what he did.

A lot of people milled about, getting things ready. Snake was off to one side, where they'd set up an office of sorts for him to take the bets. I kept going even though everything in me screamed about how bad an idea this was. When I got to the back offices near the warehouse's south side, someone emerged from the shadows, and my fists clenched until I saw who it was—Mark Rowan.

Mark had placed bets on my behalf on occasion since I started fighting. He was a known gambler who kept his trap shut. It was his only redeeming quality.

I shoved a wad of cash into his hand. "Bet on the opposition."

"Why?" He pushed his wire-rimmed glasses up on his nose, but they slipped again immediately. "Are you feeling sick? Or is your hand messed up?"

"No." I wanted to throw up. The conversation needed to end.

"Maybe you shouldn't be fighting. You haven't lost in forever. What's going on?"

"Stop with the questions," I growled, leaning down so we were eye to eye.

His left eyelid twitched.

"If you tell anyone that I bet against myself..."

He shook his head, pressing his thin lips together tightly enough that all the color leached from them. "I won't. I wouldn't ever."

"Just keep your fucking mouth shut about it, and if I lose, bring the money back to me." If he didn't, everything would go to shit.

CHAPTER TWENTY-SIX

ASPEN

The knock at my door made me jump, and a handful of Kleenexes tumbled to the ground. They were everywhere. I was sitting in a mound of them and feeling sorry for myself, which had been the status quo since the argument with Max the night before. The stupid hormones were making me unusually weepy.

I glared at the door, not making a sound. I wasn't going to open it. I looked terrible anyway, with puffy eyes and my I-don't-care-anymore outfit—my favorite black-and-teal starry pajama pants with a tear on one knee, a tight pink cami, and a gray cardigan. I was in no shape for anyone to see what a train wreck I was.

I snorted softly. My luck, it would be that jerk-off, Elias. I could only imagine the picture he would take. It would be a meme in no time and go viral with his large social media following.

I didn't understand why anyone liked him. He hid his viciousness behind sarcasm. They were all idiots.

The banging on my door grew louder, and I burrowed deeper under my comforter, which wasn't comforting me at all.

"I know you're in there, Aspen," Max shouted. "Open the door. I've got candy."

Candy? I threw the covers off and stalked to the door, flinging it open. "Damn you." I grabbed his arm, yanked him inside before anyone passing by could see me, then slammed it shut. I flipped the lock, grabbed the candy bar from his hand, then crawled back into bed. "If it wasn't for my desperate need for chocolate…"

Max glanced around, a frown on his handsome face. He looked good, as always, like James Marsden in *27 Dresses*. Of course, Max was dressed in a trendy dark-gray collared shirt and jeans, making me even more self-conscious. He kicked a path through the avalanche of Kleenexes then sat on the desk chair.

I took a bite of the chocolate and barely stifled a moan. I hadn't eaten anything more than a few crackers. It wasn't smart, but I couldn't leave the room.

"I'll take your peace offering"—I raised the chocolate in a salute—"and counter with an apology." His lips twitched, and a tiny bit of tension eased from my shoulders. "I'm sorry I barged in on your date and scared him off. Not because he didn't deserve everything I said and more, but because you shouldn't have suffered because of my outburst."

Max sighed and rolled his eyes. "I would hug you, but that whole area is contaminated."

I laughed but made no move to clean it up. I wasn't sure if he was staying or had plans with the jerk, and besides, picking up my mess would take too much effort. The teasing smile fell from his face, and I held still, waiting for what he would say.

"I'm sorry too. I shouldn't have said what I had to you. It's not—"

"True? Yeah, it kinda was." I'd had plenty of time to think about what he'd said and had reached a very unpleasant discovery. He was right. I was a selfish ass.

"Well"—he pinched his fingers together in front of him—"only a tiny bit."

"I've been so wrapped up in my problems that I haven't been a good friend. I never even asked you about Joel. What happened? I thought you liked him."

His head fell back before he responded. "I liked him too much, and he… liked Vance Jamison more."

"Ugh, that's the worst."

"I thought so. Elias was my rebound." He shrugged before standing and kicking a few white balls of ick to make a path to me. Then he picked up a book from my desk and swept the growing pile of tissues on the bed to one side before climbing up next to me and toeing his shoes off. They fell with a thump to the floor. We both scooted onto the mattress so we faced one another.

"Why've you been crying?"

"I've already made too much about me. Let's just chalk it up to hormones."

Max tucked a clump of my dirty hair behind my ear, his expression softening. "I didn't mean that. I lashed out, and it wasn't fair."

"It was." My voice was small because I felt alone and unsure. Too many things were out of my control, and while that had never bothered me that much before, it did now.

He held my hands, and the connection did more for me than all the chocolate in the world, and that was saying a lot. I was pathetic. "Tell me. I want to know."

So I did. I spilled everything about the congenital disabilities test, how I'd passed out, and how sweet Phoenix had been until he wasn't. Because he still hadn't called to see how I was doing.

"I cannot believe you didn't tell me. You know I would have gone with you."

"Yeah, but I've put a lot on you, and last night made me realize how much. Phoenix needs to step up."

"Whatever." Max rolled his eyes and pulled me in for a hug. "I'm your best friend. Don't try to deny it because I am the best, and we both know it. Next time, you confide in me. No more holding back."

"The same goes for you." I pulled back and leveled him with a reprimanding look, raising my eyebrows. "Joel?"

"You're right. New leaf, or whatever that saying is."

I laughed. "What happened with you and Elias? Has he called or spoken to you since last night?"

"No, but I haven't reached out either. You were right. He's a horrible human being. I don't need to get involved with him. There are plenty of others who want a piece of this."

"They would only be so lucky."

"Ah, see? This is why we work. My ego needs you."

"You're crazy." But I was laughing, and it felt much better than the alternative. "I'm glad you came by."

"Me too." He bopped my nose. "Now go get cleaned up. Your baby daddy is fighting tonight, and we're going to go cheer him on."

"Who's he fighting?"

"Who cares?"

He was right. I didn't. "I don't know why I even asked. You know, I never realized pregnancy brain was a real thing. I've done some weird stuff lately. At the diner, I was getting change from the register for someone who actually paid in cash, and I legit forgot how to count. Strangest thing ever—and I've always been great with money."

Max's grin widened. "Poor baby."

I rolled my eyes but was secretly okay with the sympathy. "I've just got to—"

"Shower, change into something not cringe-worthy, and brush that mop of hair."

"Okay, I look homeless. Got it." I rolled my eyes and scooted off the bed. "But you're such a diva. Who there will care what I look like?"

"You care because that smoke show will see you, and I'm saving you from self-sabotage, which you've been hell-bent on lately."

He wasn't wrong. After grabbing my bathroom stuff and some clothes, I went to take care of making myself presentable enough that Max wouldn't complain.

Even though it was petty and silly, I wanted to go so I could talk to Phoenix. He should have called to check on me. It didn't sit right that he hadn't, and I wanted to tell him that.

Max decided to drive after deciding that I looked decent enough to go out in public. When we got to the secret location, which was different from last time, it was pretty much the same, with its dimly lit interior except for the ring and the throngs of people and hard pressing of bodies that made me claustrophobic and shifted me closer to Max as he encircled me with an arm. We were in a good spot so I could see. He'd positioned me behind a few shorter girls, and no one was in front of them. We had such a good vantage point because Max had some friends who'd saved some room for us.

Fighters entered the ring and did their thing. Instead of paying attention, I searched the crowd, looking for a glimpse of Phoenix's blond head, which would have been above most of the people there. So far, no luck.

Max squeezed me against him then bent so I could hear him. "There he is."

I followed where he notched his chin. Phoenix. My breath caught in my throat. The overhead light dribbled down the washboard of his abdomen, and for a split second he was frozen at the edge of the ring, like a statue of a god. My pulse raced, thundering against my eardrums. He bent then slid through the ropes and into the ring.

My mind replayed a slice of being with him at the cove, and

my lips tingled with the memory of every kiss he had ever given me. His expression was determined, as always, with his brows set straight across his forehead and his jaw flexed.

Something was different, though. His expression was off. He looked… defeated, wary. Maybe apprehensive. I didn't know who he was fighting, but my stomach twisted because if he was worried, then so was I. I let out the breath I was holding as he bounced on his toes, warming up, shaking his arms out, just like I'd seen him do before every fight.

The announcer did his thing, and the fighters circled each other. Phoenix threw the first punch, and the other guy's head snapped back from the power behind it. A thrill raced through me. I wouldn't admit it, but holy hell, it affected me in the most primal way.

When Phoenix turned to look at someone in the crowd, the other guy sucker-punched him then followed with a three-punch combination. My blood turned to ice as he took punches he could have blocked. He took a wide swing and missed. Even his kicks didn't land with maximum impact.

The crowd sensed something was off, too, and quickly reached pandemonium levels. Max positioned me so I was protected in front of him with two of his friends at my sides when he motioned them close.

Something's wrong. I couldn't shake the sense of dread that consumed me. Fear licked up my spine as another hit landed on Phoenix's jaw, and he stumbled back then down to a knee. He didn't get it. The announcer counted him off. When he rose after the fight was called, he swayed, almost falling over.

My eyes misted with tears. I had to make sure he was okay. I tugged on Max's arm. "We have to go to the back. I need to see him."

His friends shifted, and I dragged Max through the crowd, which was already engaged in watching the next fight. When we made it to the hallway that led to the locker rooms, or the space they use for changing and getting ready, I caught a glimpse of a big blond guy in a group of three large men. I recognized Phoenix, Shane, and an older version of them. He had to have been their dad.

Shane and Phoenix were yelling at each other. Phoenix pushed Shane into the wall then went into the room and slammed the door so hard it sounded like the roof would collapse.

We inched forward as Shane followed his brother. The older man just stood there, and I didn't understand why—it seemed like he should try to stop his sons from killing each other.

"We shouldn't be here." Max took my wrist and tried to pull me back.

I shook him off. "I need to be here." I couldn't explain it, but something was wrong, and I had to help Phoenix. I rushed toward the door, stepped in front of their dad, and shoved it open. I took one step inside before pain exploded in my head and the world went black.

CHAPTER TWENTY-SEVEN

PHOENIX

Holy fuck! Goddammit, Shane. I swung at him. He'd ducked. My fist hit Aspen, and she crumpled. Shane pivoted fast, grabbing her at the same time as Max. They'd kept her from hitting the ground. But my world had already crashed and burned.

I hit Aspen. Fear had me in a chokehold. All I could think about was what I'd done and how hurt she could be. I took Aspen from Shane and Max, who resisted at first, and cradled her body to my chest. The punch had been meant for Shane and had come with some power.

I held her close and glared at my brother. I couldn't believe that cocksucker brought our fucking dad to the fights. If anything happened to Aspen… I couldn't go there.

Max was the first to speak. "She should go to the hospital."

I clipped a nod. He was right. "Where's your car, Shane?" He could drive so I could hold her. I needed to feel her in my arms and take care of her. *I fucking hurt her.* It hadn't been my intent, but the damage was done. Blood leaked in a small stream from her nose, which was swelling. A hint of darkness shadowed her eyes.

"My Jeep is close to the side door," our sperm donor said.

"I'll meet you there." Max had already turned and was dashing in the opposite direction, probably to where he'd parked. I saw the judgment on his face. It didn't matter. Nothing but Aspen being okay mattered. He must have had the same thought.

We burst through the door. I felt very little of the damp, cold air but couldn't help but worry that she felt everything. I tried to pull her closer, wanting to share my body heat with her.

Darkness enveloped most of the parking lot except for a few scattered streetlamps. I couldn't look at my asshole father. Rage simmered beneath fear. My focus had to be on Aspen. I would deal with him and Shane when I knew she was okay, safe and away from whatever fucked-up family reunion this was supposed to be.

She weighed almost nothing. I carried her out the side door to my asshole father's Jeep, which wasn't far. Shane grabbed the roll bar and climbed into the front. I sat in the back, holding Aspen. I wasn't sure I would be able to let her go when we got to the hospital. The doctors would probably have to pry her from my arms.

Shane directed the asshole, and we zoomed through the parking lot. I didn't pay attention, refusing even to look at him. Instead, I kept saying her name, begging her to wake up.

Fuck! I couldn't even tell if she was breathing. Panic raged through me. I didn't know what to do.

"Put your ear to her mouth!" Shane shouted, twisting around in his seat. "You'll be able to hear or feel if she's breathing."

"There's too much wind." We whipped around corners, and he floored it down straightaways. It didn't matter how fast we went or that we were weaving through cars like crazy people. She needed help. The light ahead turned yellow. *Come on. Faster.* "Get us to the hospital!"

We were a few blocks away, and he blew the light. A boom

sounded as the Jeep jolted brutally. Everything happened at once. We spun. Shane was there one minute but gone the next. I shoved Aspen beneath me and threw myself on top of her, holding the seat in a death grip to stay where we were.

Two more hits. The Jeep did a one-eighty. Metal collided with metal. I shielded Aspen's body as best as I could. Pain exploded in my head. We bounced off whatever we'd hit or had hit us again then came to a halt. But my head didn't stop spinning. I could make out only my dad slumped over the windshield and the feeling of Aspen's warm body safely beneath mine.

Where's Shane?

Is it raining? Why is my face wet? I tried to yell for help, but no sound came out. My head bobbed forward. I couldn't hold it up. My face landed in Aspen's soft hair, and I blinked until everything went black.

Want to know what happens between Phoenix and Aspen? To find out, continue reading the Hidden Valley Elite series with Cruel Love.

If you enjoyed reading CRUEL HATE as much as I did writing it, I hope you'll consider leaving a review.

ABOUT THE AUTHOR

Isla Vaughn is the author of the Hidden Valley Elite series. Her romance books are full of complex characters, strong alpha males, and the fierce women who bring them to their knees. When not writing, she can be found daydreaming about owning a beach house, reading, or drinking too much coffee.

instagram.com/islavaughnauthor
goodreads.com/islavaughn_author
bookbub.com/profile/isla-vaughn
x.com/IVaughn_Author
facebook.com/author.IslaVaughn
tiktok.com/@islavaughnauthor

ALSO BY ISLA VAUGHN

Hidden Valley Elite Series

Savage Start

Savage Lies

Savage Truth

Brutal Days

Brutal Nights

Cruel Start

Cruel Hate

Cruel Love

Wicked Games

Wicked Ends